OAK ISLAND

A FLINT MCQUAID ADVENTURE

A NOVEL BY
MAX WALDER

OAK ISLAND: A FLINT MCQUAID ADVENTURE

WWW.SEVEREDPRESS.COM

ISBN: 978-1-922861-75-7

For Desmond Floyd
The greatest adventurer I know.

PROLOGUE

Egypt, Summer 1920

Flint McQuaid wiped the sweat from his stinging eyes and watched as his father Nolan effortlessly scaled the slope of the pyramid. Declan, his half-brother, moved behind him with almost as much simple grace. Two mountain goats on a journey together. Flint swore and spat sand at his feet.

He watched as Declan hammered in a new climbing bolt between the seams of the pyramid's great stones. He wondered to himself how the two of them had gotten so good at climbing together while living in Paris. From everything Flint had read, Paris was a hotbed of culture and art, not a place one would go bouldering in. He considered Paris to be an intellectual paradise compared to Winston-Salem, North Carolina, where he lived with his mother.

She didn't like to talk about his father, so Flint had never really understood what had brought the two professors who had borne him to the rural place. He did, however, understand his desire to leave it. He just wished he could wrap his mind and his heart around why his father hadn't thought to take his family with him when he did.

Maybe, he thought as he watched Declan follow his father nimbly up the pyramid's face, it had been about Declan all along. Maybe he had simply been practice for his father to finally get it right with a beautiful German woman and their brilliant son.

As near as he could tell, the only things he really shared with Declan were the strong jaw and mahogany brown hair that they had both inherited from their father.

"Boy!" Nolan shouted down the sloping stone surface. His voice was a deep baritone that comforted Flint at the same time that it made him uneasy. "Pick up the pace! We're almost there and we're burning away what remains of our daylight."

"Yes, Father," Flint called back.

He ignored Declan's smirking smile as he dug into the rock face with the climbing hobnails on the bottom of his boots and forced his legs to move him upward. His muscles burned almost as much as his skin beneath the blazing sun. He was embarrassed at his lack of energy and skill. He was sixteen, the perfect age to be capable of this adventurous work. Yet he was being outshone by his thirteen-year-old half-brother and forty-year-old father.

He pushed these thoughts from his mind and instead made himself focus on the promise of what was hidden within the pyramid. Gold and jewels, yes. But it was the other possibilities that excited Flint: Ancient scrolls depicting thrilling adventures, beautifully carved furniture, artwork unlike any he had seen in dreary North Carolina. He had spent countless hours at home reading the pulp stories and poring over the archaeological tomes his father had left behind.

When he'd received the letter from Nolan inviting him to take part in the "family trip", as he'd called hit, no amount of warning from his mother could have stopped him. Now he was finally nearing the big moment. He pushed himself harder and faster, closing the gap between himself and the two men he called family.

They climbed for another twenty feet or so before Nolan suddenly stopped. He held up his hand in a wordless signal. His two boys immediately froze in place.

"This is it," Nolan announced with firm confidence.

Flint hustled upward until he reached the other two.

"Eight blocks in, thirteen blocks up. All adding up to seven times three," his father continued.

Flint at the stone blocks surrounding them, coating the surface of the pyramid in a grid-like pattern. Perfect for both demarking and obscuring secret entryways.

"Right where that guide in the market said it would be," Declan murmured.

"His name was Sadiki, I think," Flint said.

The other two stared at him for a minute before Declan said, "It doesn't matter. You can't trust those people. He told us because we paid him."

"Your brother is right," Nolan said. Then he asked with a sudden sharpness, "Declan my boy, what does the number seven represent in Egyptian mythology?"

Without hesitation, Declan answered. "It represented the concept of perfection and completeness. This is why the hieroglyphic symbol for gold contains seven spines."

"Excellent. Flint. What is the meaning behind the number three?"

Flint stammered. Even beneath his sunburn his embarrassed blush was visible.

"I, uh, well. I don't know."

Declan snorted a laugh. Nolan ignored him.

"Three is the basic symbol for plurality. Hence, the triads of Gods, which I'm sure you know about."

"Yeah sure, of course," Flint lied.

"Very good."

Nolan dropped to one knee, careful to keep his balance against the sloping side of the pyramid. He removed a small brush from the leather satchel hanging from his belt and began to brush years of sand away from the surface of the stone. Little by little, he unearthed a symbol.

Two arms, connected in a ‘u’ shape, as if a person was holding up arms crooked at 90-degree angles. Only there was no person, just the two arms running seamlessly from one into the other. It was faintly carved, impossible to see from the ground. Only visible to those who already knew where they were going.

“The symbol of *ka*. The soul. This is it. This is where Tutankhamun was laid to rest.”

Both boys listened to him in rapt attention. A massive grin spread across Nolan’s face and Flint felt excitement well up in his belly.

“Boys, I have an idea. Each of you place a palm over one of the hands. Then push gently. Open the doorway together.”

Immediately, Declan crouched on the right side of the stone, and placed his hand over the hieroglyphs. From the left side, Flint moved to do the same, but Declan quickly put his hand down and began to push against the carving as hard as he could. Flint pulled back, wounded.

Nolan laughed and exclaimed, “Cheeky boy!” Turing to Flint, he said, “You’ll have to be quicker in the future, son. Remember that.”

The stone moved easily inward with the grinding sound of stone on stone. Sand poured out from between the cracks as the stone fell into the pyramid, revealing a pitch-black maw behind it.

Flint gazed into the darkness. At the same time that his stomach began to churn with apprehension, he felt a strange pull. He was drawn to seek out the secrets inside.

“Well…” Nolan intoned, his voice even deeper than usual. “As much as I would like to be the first person to set foot inside Tutankhamun’s tomb, perhaps one of my sons would like to?”

Flint ignored the urge to ask if they were the first to enter who had put the good king there in the first place and instead breathlessly said, "I'll do it! I'll go in first."

Both Nolan and Declan stared at Flint; Nolan with a look of bemused surprise, Declan with a glare, his eyes narrowed slits of anger.

"Well. Alright then," Nolan said and clapped his son on the shoulder. "Let's see what kind of man you've become. Show us your mettle, Flint."

It was the first time Flint remembered his father touching him outside of a firm handshake when he'd first gotten off the boat in Alexandria Port. He smiled and said, "Yes sir."

He reached into the canvas rucksack on his back and removed a wooden torch. Next, he pulled out a mason jar full of clear liquid. Gasoline. Before he could open it, Nolan put his hand over the lid.

"Not so fast, boy," Nolan said. "You can do that inside, put it back."

His son complied. Without another word, Nolan took a length of climbing rope strung over his shoulder and ran the rope through the metal rings in their belts, stopping to tie each one in a hitch knot. They were connected. A single organism.

"Now climb on down. Investigate to make sure it's safe. We'll follow you in. And don't touch anything. Egyptians were crafty. They filled their tombs with traps to ward off grave robbers and the like."

Flint took a deep breath and crawled into the hole. As soon as he entered, he found himself in total darkness. He steeled his nerves and crawled on. After a couple of knee-scuffing feet, he suddenly tumbled out into the chilled, stale air of the tomb. He swore as he tumbled onto the carved block they had just pushed inside and then landed on the floor.

He winced and clutched the elbow he had landed on. It would hurt like hell in the morning, but that was a problem for later. He didn't want his father or, worse, snide little Declan, to hear him whine.

Struggling in the darkness, he pulled the torch and mason jar from his pack. As he opened the jar he fumbled in the dark and let the lid roll away into the shadows. He dipped the end of the torch into the open jar and let the gasoline soak into the fabric. He removed a box of matches from his pocket and lit one.

"Ah, Blue Diamond," he said to no one in particular.

He ignited the torch and suddenly the world was alight and alive. He took a deep breath. Over the smell of the burning gasoline, all he could get was musty air. Appropriate for a tomb, he thought. Examining the dimly lit world around him, he was disappointed to see that it was all fairly nondescript stone and dirt.

He moved about the space and quickly realized that it was little more than a small box, roughly ten feet by twelve feet, with a ceiling high enough for Flint's six-foot-tall frame. The uneven roughness of the stone above him meant he had to be careful to not scrape his head.

No hallways, no doors, no stairwells. The place was little more than a cell.

The rope tugged at his belt. Nolan's voice called down through the hole. "What do you see, boy?"

"Um… nothing, basically," he said.

"I'm going to need you to elaborate on that a bit," Nolan said.

Declan's snicker echoed down into the tomb.

Then something caught his eye. A carving in the stone wall. As he moved closer his torch illuminated it through the room's dusty haze. The carving depicted two crisscrossed knives suspended over an open palm. It reminded Flint of a pirate's skull and crossbones. There was something threatening about it, and it excited him as much as it frightened him.

"Wait, I think I have something," he called to the outside.

He could hear Declan begin to scramble through the hole, then heard their father say, "No son, wait until we know it's safe."

Taking the opportunity to do what Declan had robbed from him, he reached out and placed his open palm against that of the carving. His was a bit larger, but the carving was receptive to his touch. As soon as he put some force behind it, the hand began to withdraw into the stone wall. Flint watched in wide-eyed fascination.

Then the floor beneath fell away and he was falling into a deep, dark void.

He dropped about six feet before the rope caught him and pulled tight. The torch flew from his hand and tumbled down until it disappeared. He was suspended in the darkness.

Flint looked upward to find that his father and half-brother were hanging on the same line over the tomb's open floor, illuminated by the sharp lines of the sun beaming through the square hole. Declan was screaming. It was so high-pitched Flint would have laughed had he not been swinging over certain death.

Nolan was curiously silent. All that Flint could hear from him were a few deep breaths. Huff, huff, huff.

Then, their father said, "Boys. A bit of bad news."

"It gets worse?!" Declan hollered.

"I'm afraid so."

"What is it, Dad?" Flint asked. He wasn't panicking. He knew his father would have the answer. He would get them out of this.

"The climbing bolt that has us anchored, it's… coming loose. It can't support all of our weight."

Flint's eyes darted around the murky darkness. On the far wall to his right, there was a small ledge.

"If I swing out, I think I can grab a hold to the wall over there," he called out.

He began to sway back and forth. Declan let out a little panicked whine.

"Stop it, boy!" Nolan's voice was stern. Angry. "You're loosening the bolt even more; we're all about to drop."

"What are we going to do?" cried Declan.

"Don't worry, Declan." But Declan was hyperventilating. Nolan spoke to him softly, calmly. A stark contrast to the way he'd just addressed Flint. "Declan, son. Calm down. Take a deep breath. That's good. Now, reach into the utility pouch on your belt. Take out the thing I got you for Christmas."

Flint watched from below as Declan, sniffling, rooted around in a pouch on his belt and removed something. He watched as his brother flicked that something open to reveal a knife blade, sharp and glinting in the dull light. A sick dread churned his guts.

Flint said, "What… what are you going to do with that knife, Declan?"

But Declan didn't know the answer either and so both boys simply stared up at their father, mouths slack with curious expectation.

"I'm sorry, Flint," Nolan said. "But the bolt can't hold all the weight. We have to lighten the load, or we'll all die. At least this way your brother has a chance."

"Wha- What? No, please! Declan, don't do it.

"And I told you not to touch anything down there, didn't I?" Nolan asked sharply.

Flint's words caught in his throat. He couldn't speak.

"Cut it, Declan." When the boy hesitated, Nolan said, "Don't be a coward. Do it. *Now*."

Tears streamed down the boy's face as he began to saw into the rope. Back and forth, back and forth. He was surprisingly methodical.

Flint felt his weight pull him further down as the rope began to thin, one braided strand at a time. Something warm and wet fell on his face and hands. His brother's tears.

Before the rope snapped and he fell into the black, he heard the boy whisper, "I'm sorry."

***

When Flint came to, he felt the flickering warmth of a flame near his face. The world was nothing but fluttering shadows. He sat up. Blinked his eyes. His vision began to clear. Then the pain hit.

His whole body hurt, but it was the throbbing in his head and piercing pain on his chin that really did a number on him. Instinctively he touched his chin and came away with blood covering his hand. It was then he realized he had a gash at least an inch long and his neck was slick with the blood flowing out.

Flint stumbled to his feet. Blood trickled out into the sand covering the stone floor. Shockingly, his torch hadn't gone out in the fall and was still burning on the ground. At least he hadn't tumbled on top of it and burnt alive.

"Lucky me," he muttered to himself and picked up the torch.

He waved it slowly around the space, trying to get his bearings. In the murky dark he made out four walls, surrounding him on all sides. The room was so small that he didn't think he could even lay down in it. The ceiling was barely a foot above his head.

I'm trapped, he thought. *In a very, very small space.*

His pulse suddenly quickened. His breath came in short, sharp inhales. A fear he'd never known gripped him.

Such a small space.

He closed his eyes tightly. He forced his breathing to slow. He took long, deep breaths and slowly his pulse went down as well. He pushed back the fear into the recesses of his mind. He didn't have room for fear. He had to figure his way out of this place. There had to be a way. There just had to be. He opened his eyes.

Using the wan light of his torch, he examined the walls. The enormous bricks were held tight. Not a single crack, no slivers of light peeking out. Working his way around the base of the room was just as fruitless. The walls were snug to the sandy floor.

Then he saw it. A bit of sand trickling down from the top of a brick. It had to be coming from the outside, blown into the cracks between bricks by the windy desert. He explored the edges of the brick, running his fingers delicately around the grooves, careful not to set off another trap.

The other bricks were perfectly sealed with no space at all between them. However, this brick space had just a millimeter or two between itself and its partners. *Perhaps it was looser for a reason. Perhaps they designed it to move.* He tried not to get too excited.

He cleared the sand from the grooves. Beneath the dirt, distinct cracks ran at both the top of the stone and the top of the one beneath it. Or at least they looked like cracks at first. He leaned in, took a closer look in the flickering light of his torch. There was something… intentional about the cracks. Looking at the top cracks on the brick below, he realized that if they were put together the lines would connect.

"But how…?" he murmured to himself.

As he looked more closely at the edges of the stone he noticed that his torch was dying. That also meant that oxygen was lowering in the tiny space. He didn't have much time. He remembered then how small his little tomb was and the panic began to rise again in his chest. At a loss, he placed his hand on the stone and pushed.

For a moment, nothing happened. Then, he heard the grind of stone on stone. The front of the brick moved forward, revealing that it was actually a separate stone plate. It emerged from between the other bricks and then slowly rotated one-hundred-and-eighty degrees. It then pulled back into the wall until it was flush once more.

Flint examined the bottom seam of the brick. The cracks were now aligned, and he discovered that he had been right. They weren't cracks at all. They were hieroglyphic letters. At first, they meant nothing. He racked his brain, remembering the books his father had left behind. Letter by letter, he broke it down until a single word formed before him.

<u>Lucky</u>

He pushed against the surface of the stone once more, and this time it moved backward as a single piece. It continued as if by magic, grinding against the sand and stone until sunlight began to peek around its edges. Flint watched in amazement as it finally tumbled out of the other side and the harsh rays of the desert sun nearly blinded him. He dropped the torch and climbed through the hole on his hands and knees.

He emerged into the world, and, in that moment, nothing had ever felt better than the warm, dry air on his skin. He laughed when he looked down and realized that he wasn't more than ten feet from the sandy earth.

An hour later he arrived at camp, exhausted and dehydrated. Declan and Nolan were enjoying a plate of fruit and fresh ice water. They stared at him in shock as he approached. Flint walked up to the table, took the pitcher of water, and never spoke to them again.

CHAPTER 1

The boulder was coming. Fast.

The man raised his grizzled countenance from beneath his fedora and quickly assessed the situation. *Not ideal*, he decided.

"Looks like the treasure of Yum Kaax will have to wait," he muttered gruffly, adding a sarcastic edge just for himself.

He turned on a dime and sprinted back the way he'd come, the only entrance into the ancient cave temple, pinning his hat down tight with one hand, gripping his Webley revolver in the other. His feet danced nimbly over the loose rock that littered the temple floors like the worst carpeting in history. He leapt over a small pit, the one that had mortally claimed his guide, Elvio, only moments before.

"Godspeed, Elvio," he called out as he launched over the pit.

Looking over his shoulder he saw the boulder, perfectly spherical, wasn't slowing its attack. If anything, it had gotten even faster. Eyes narrowed in determination, he kicked up his knees and floored it. Sweat began to pour down his face, obscuring his vision. He wiped his eyes clean just in time to see the heavy vine hanging in front of him. Too late.

The vine caught him around the throat and suspended him a moment, his still running feet left kicking in the air before he slammed down into the dirt on his back. He let out a desperate gasp as the wind was knocked out of him. For a moment he struggled to get up, but knew it was hopeless. The boulder was practically upon him already.

"Goodnight, sweet prince," he said to himself.

He let his body go slack. He closed his eyes tight. He would die with dignity. A second later, the boulder rolled over him and continued on down the rocky path.

For a moment all was still. Then, the man raised his head and spoke.

"Goddamn it, that vine really hurt my throat. Can we get set dec in here?"

"Cut!" a voice called out.

"That's a cut!" a second voice echoed.

The eager whirr of the camera suddenly came to a stop.

Los Angeles, CA 1935

The man marched off of the set of the Mayan temple, slapping his now-soiled fedora on his leg.

The director, Michael, approached him with a huge fake smile slapped across his face. "Clark, that was beautiful! I know the end didn't quite work out, but-"

"My throat! My throat! Are there red markings, Michael? Where is makeup?"

Away from the two chattering men, away from the bustling film crew struggling to get the boulder back in position, in the shadows beyond the harsh movie lights, Flint watched. A bemused grin flickered across his face, watching as the conversation turned into an argument. Something about an inability to capture human truth in action. He rolled his eyes. It was all so silly.

At least the stone carvings adorning the temple walls were accurate. He had seen to that. The picture, *The Vanished Empire*, had been just about to start rolling when Flint had been assigned to act as a historical advisor on the film. Most of the studios in town didn't care much for cultural or historical accuracy, but the Head of Development at Horizon Pictures, Noah Weissbaum, was a stickler. He'd never explained just why to Flint, but Flint hadn't bothered to ask once he saw the dollar amount listed on his contract. He'd signed on with Horizon and Weissbaum, bought himself a Beverly Hills bungalow with a nice little pool, and never looked back.

From somewhere in the shadows, he heard a heavy sigh. He found the source: Callie Carver, the writer of *The Vanished Empire*. She was slouched back in a canvas director's chair, her boots resting heavily on the wooden footrest. He'd never seen a screenwriter quite as protective of their words. Most guys were in and out and on to the next movie, but not Callie. She was monitoring every line, every detail, and speaking up when someone tried to change them. Unfortunately for Flint, that meant she'd been up his ass about everything from the engravings in ancient coins to changes in the food prepared by the Mayans. To her it was all about symbolism and subtext. To him, and more importantly to Weissbaum, if it was wrong, it was wrong.

He'd tried to ignore her whenever they were in proximity on set, but she was hard to look away from. She was pretty, he supposed, but it wasn't her full lips or sculpted aquiline nose or high cheek bones. No, he didn't care anything about that, he reminded himself. It was everything else about her. She was six feet tall with long, flaming red hair pulled back in a tight ponytail. Her wardrobe was full of what he assumed were actually women's clothes, but were always pants, long shirts, and leather jackets. Never a dress, no jewelry that he could see. She was always conspicuously covered from her ankles to her wrists. She almost made him self-conscious about his own innate sense of style. His pocket squares and bold ties. His perfectly groomed, dark brown pencil mustache. His fondness for velvet blazers. *God, she's annoying*, he thought.

Then, he caught himself wondering how tall Callie would be in a pair of high heels… He stopped himself.

"She could punch my lights out," he said to himself and snickered.

He watched as she sighed again, louder this time, and then walked over to where Clark and Michael were bickering. She immediately began pointing at a line in the script which made Michael even more frustrated. Sensing some amusing drama, Flint decided to make himself useful. He tapped a cigarette out from a silver case, lit up, and headed over.

He arrived just in time to hear Michael say to Callie, "Before I worked with all of you, my pictures went smooth as silk! Like eggs in coffee, every time. Now, every five seconds one of you is giving me guff, and yes that includes you, Flint." The director looked at him impatiently. "I assume you've discovered a new archaeological ineptitude?"

He looked to Callie and then back to Michael. He couldn't resist. "A rolling boulder? That's not even possible."

"And why not?"

"How would they get a boulder perfectly spherical like that?" He wasn't one hundred percent with that one, but he went for it.

"How do you know?" she shot back.

"Oh, I don't know, years of actual archaeological fieldwork all over the world."

She eyed him up and down, sizing him up. "I know all about your fieldwork, Mr. McQuaid. People talk. Graduate school at Harvard, then three years digging up bones, then seven years lounging around Hollywoodland 'advising' artists and bedding chorus girls."

He had to hand it to her, she'd done her homework. "That's seven years bedding chorus girls. I'm only thirty-five."

She eyed his tailored suit. His alligator skin shoes. "Sure you are, fancy pants."

Fancy pants? He didn't know what to say to that, but he didn't want to lose face, so he turned his attention to Clark who had been standing there, slack jawed, the entire time. "Is anyone gonna mention that Clark's five o'clock shadow is painted on?"

He reached out and swiped a finger across Clark's cheek, coming away with brown makeup on his fingertip and leaving behind a stripe of bare skin.

"You horse's ass!" Clark shouted. "She's right, you look like a fairy!"

"Hey! Uncalled for! And not for nothing, no judgment here, but wasn't that you basketeering the night away at Beery's house party on Friday night?"

Clark's face flushed with rage. "You're a heel," he said. He turned to their director who was rubbing his temples with his thumbs, eyes closed. "I'll be in my dressing room, Michael. Goodbye, Miss Carver."

Clark hurried away, pushing past a grip, and nearly knocking him over.

"He's right you know; you are a heel. That wasn't right," Callie said.

"I'm sorry!" Flint called after Clark, but the actor ignored him. To Michael he said, "I meant that, by the way. I am sorry. But he is an ass."

Michael ignored him. Instead, he turned to Callie and curtly said, "Callie. You were next. What do you want?"

Instead of saying anything, she simply pointed to Doug, the actor playing the hero's companion, Elvio. Doug, while a competent enough bit player and Flint's favorite bartender at the Frolic Room, was white. In order to play Elvio, he was covered head to toe in olive makeup and sporting a slicked back black wig. Doug, sitting on the edge of the stage, was preoccupied with rebuilding a ham sandwich that had fallen apart in his lap and didn't notice the new attention.

"What?" Michael asked. "It's fucking Doug, so what?"

"He doesn't remotely look like a Mayan. Surely, we can get a real Hispanic actor on set."

"I don't know how to answer that right now, Callie. Flint, what do you want?" The director was waving.

"I actually agree with her. Doug's a great guy, but whatever that is, it isn't working. Plus, from my point of view, it is rather historically inaccurate, Mike."

"Thank you," Callie said. Flint thought he heard a begrudging edge to the comment. "For God's sake we're in Los Angeles, Michael."

"I'll take you up to Boyle Heights right now and pick up some high school theatre kid that'll work circles around Doug." Flint looked over at the potbellied man picking a tomato slice up off of the floor. "No offense, Doug."

Doug shrugged.

Callie turned on Flint, "I don't think we need to go kidnapping high school kids. Unless you're looking for a date."

"Would you lay off? Christ Almighty, I'm agreeing with you, Big Red."

"We don't all have dads who can get us into Harvard," she quipped back.

Flint's face suddenly turned stony. His voice was measured but firm. "Don't talk about my father."

Callie clammed up. She arched an eyebrow at Michael, who gave an uncomfortable shrug.

"Fine. I won't," she said finally.

Michael was back to rubbing his temples. "Look, whatever this little team up thing is that you two are doing, I can't handle it right now. At least for today, the picture is what the picture is. I have to go trick an actor into leaving his dressing room."

As Callie and Flint watched him march away, an awkward silence fell over the two of them. The feeling that he was being watched suddenly washed over Flint. He looked over his shoulder to find Weissbaum standing in the shadows at the edge of the stage. He was indeed watching Flint. Or Callie. Or both of them. Flint couldn't be sure. The man's presence always made Flint feel insecure. His boss' custom tailored Viennese suits, always pinstripe, put even Flint's wardrobe to shame, and the studio head's serious demeanor made him uneasy.

Weissbaum caught Flint looking back at him but didn't turn away. He just continued to stare. There was something in his gaze that Flint had never seen before. The man almost looked worried. *But that was impossible*, Flint told himself. The man was a stone-cold executive. Hollywoodland, through and through. Noah Weissbaum didn't get worried. Even if he did look like it.

Unsettled, Flint turned back to Callie as he whispered, "Hey, you ever get the feeling Weissbaum is-"

But Callie was gone. Flint had been left all alone. He kicked at a cable on the floor and took a drag off his cigarette.

What he didn't tell her, what he would never tell her, was that for all she knew about him, he had tried to uncover the same. He'd found nothing. Callie was right, people did talk. Normally everyone on the studio lot was constantly gossiping, sharing stories about anyone from

Claudette Colbert to the kid getting coffees, but nobody seemed to know where she came from, nor how she had muscled through the boys to become a solo screenwriter. She was hiding something, and he didn't like it. He didn't like her.

Looking back, he saw Weissbaum had vanished as well. He shivered.

Between Callie and Weissbaum, there was entirely too much mystery for Flint's liking.

CHAPTER 2

"Cannonball!" Evelyn yelled just before leaping into the pool.

Flint had tried to pull his lounge chair far enough away from the pool, but flecks of water still caught him and his newspaper. He hadn't exactly wanted Evelyn and her friend, what's-her-name, to come over that day. It was the day after the dust up on the set of *The Vanished Empire.* It was normal to get a little snippy on-set, but he was doubtful that Clark would ever talk to him again, which was a shame because Clark had some of the best party favor connections in town. Besides, he was a fun guy in general.

But it wasn't Clark that weighed especially heavy on his mind. It was Weissbaum. His presence on set that day was abnormal, and Flint couldn't shake the look he'd given him. There was no way that his fighting with Callie had resembled anything remotely professional.

Callie. Weissbaum had to see that she'd started everything. At least, that's what Flint hoped. That woman could be so damned irritating. Always picking at him, and for what? It didn't make sense. Why had she done all that digging on him? Why had he tried to find out about her? He didn't know why he was drawn to know more, and it bothered him. There was the obvious, that she was a woman flying solo in a position that she wouldn't have normally been in, but that didn't bother him like it did some. Curious, yes. But troubling? No. There was something else…

"Flint!"

Evelyn snapped Flint out of his reverie. He put down the paper to find the script girl at the edge of the pool, her head resting on her arms, her legs kicking lazily in the water. She smiled at him with dazzling pearly whites. Her wet blonde hair glistened in the California sun. Everything about her was glowing. Evelyn was a joy and Flint was struck with the idea that he was a very lucky man.

She laughed at him and said, "You just had the dreamiest, big-eyed expression on your face. Like a wheat who just got off the bus looking for the Hollywoodland sign."

He snorted a laugh but didn't crack a smile.

"Aw, poor baby," Evelyn said. "You're a sensitive boy, I should have been more delicate."

"It's not that, Evie. It's… I don't know, I had a strange day yesterday."

She rose from the pool and sat down on the lounge chair next to him. She put her hand on his. They had learned each other's preferred physical languages. When to engage, when not to. They had dated off and on for about a year but had eventually decided to remain just friends. Unless there was a particularly gin-soaked evening and then, every once in a while, they went back in time together for a moment, before waking up in the present. Flint was grateful for her friendship and counsel.

"There was a lot of drama and… I didn't help things. Weissbaum saw. I think he has it out for me now."

"Oh, Flint. I'm sure you did more than not help."

This time he smiled.

"If it makes you feel better, I've heard that set has been certifiably wacky. I'm so grateful I got put on *Lottie's Big Day* instead. Too many egos over there. Not just yours." She gave his hand a squeeze. "Why, just the other day Doris was telling me- Oh! Where's Doris?"

They looked around the pool for Doris, the young woman that Evelyn had brought with her that afternoon for a dip and a drink. A makeup artist and new friend that Evelyn had recently met on the set of a romance picture.

"I'll find her, you get back to having fun. Thank you, Evie."

Flint rose and gave Evelyn a quick peck on the forehead, then walked inside the house.

The two-bedroom bungalow was small, but modern and cozy. Despite being filled with a well-curated collection of artifacts and curios from around the world, the place was neat. Flint always kept the place tidy, the way that ladies preferred. He had overcome his baser instincts to meet their expectations and they usually seemed pleasantly shocked.

First, he went to the bathroom. The door was closed. He knocked.

"Hello? Doris? You know we have a much bigger pool in the backyard."

No answer.

He moved down the hallway and peered into his study. It was meant to be used as a guest bedroom, but he had no family visiting from out of town. He had taken the opportunity to turn the room into a private office, filled with the academic library he needed to do his work. A cot folded up in the closet would do if someone ever needed to stay the night in a bed other than his own. He gave the room a quick pass, then closed it behind him.

That only left the bedroom. As he crept quietly toward the door, it occurred to him that he had no idea who this young woman was and yet he allowed her into his home. It occurred to him that he may be an idiot.

When he stepped into the room he saw her, standing at the far wall, examining something hung there. The hardwood floor creaked under his foot and startled Doris. She turned quickly and faced him. A flirtatious smile played on her red lips. She was hiding something behind her back.

"Hey, Doris. If you're looking for my diary I keep it locked up, sorry."

"I didn't mean to intrude," she said. "I really like your decorations. All the masks and sculptures."

She was wearing a two-piece bathing suit. The kind Dolores Del Rio had recently shocked the nation with in *Flying Down to Rio*. Doris' high-waisted shorts clung to her hips and her midriff still glistened with the slightest remnants of pool water. Flint's gaze moved from her to the bed in between them. *You are an idiot*, he reminded himself.

She said, "I was thinking…if Evelyn's busy, maybe we could have some fun together."

He tried to ignore her smiling lips, her round, rosy face, all framed with a head of lustrous black hair. Somehow her hair seemed perfectly dried and styled, despite the pool. He was impressed.

Instead of saying what he wanted to, he said, "Aw, I don't know, Doris. We don't wanna leave ol' Evie waiting out there. She's our friend."

Her eyes ignited with a gleam of wicked excitement. "Oh, come on, Doctor McQuaid! Let's pretend we're in the movies…"

She brandished a mask from behind her back. An 18th century Venetian bauta mask. All white and nearly featureless save for the two eye holes. It had a large triangular jaw that swept out at the bottom, giving it an imposing look. She slipped it over her head and let out a muffled giggle. When the mask was made it was designed as a mask of seduction for the wealthy to play in. That day, worn by Doris in his bungalow, it was just a little creepy. That wasn't what bothered Flint most though.

"Doris, you're a stitch, but that mask is around two hundred years old and was owned by the writer Giovanni Grevembroch himself. It's incredibly valuable, historically. I need you to take that off now."

Her hands drifted upward, but instead of removing the mask, they stopped at the top of her two piece.

"Nope, that's not what I need you to take off." Flint moved to take the mask off himself but was stopped when his bedside phone rang.

Both of them stood, frozen for a moment, shocked at the presence of another interrupting their weirdly intimate moment. Then Flint sighed, trudged over to the phone, and picked it up.

Gruffly, he said, "Who is this? It's my day off."

The voice on the end of the line didn't introduce itself. It didn't have to. The voice simply told him where to be and when. Then it hung up. Flint was still holding the phone receiver limply in his hand when Evelyn walked in and stopped in her tracks. She took in the scene: Flint looking a bit dumbfounded, Doris wearing nothing but the mask and her two piece.

"Oh, hi Evelyn," Doris said nervously.

Evelyn's look was a mix of amusement and judgment. "What's going on here? Who's on the phone?"

Flint hung up the phone and plopped down on the bed, defeated. He turned to his friend and said, "First of all, nothing at all. Second, it's Weissbaum. He wants to see me in his office. On a Saturday."

***

Weissbaum's office was nearly as big as Flint's two bedroom bungalow. Flint flopped back on the enormous sofa in what he liked to call the living room area of his boss' office: a sofa and several overstuffed leather chairs in a semi-circle around a fireplace that always seemed to be going, even in the Los Angeles summer.

Flint scanned the room again to make sure that he was alone. Weissbaum's secretary had led him in and then left him to his own devices. After pouring himself a scotch he had flopped down on the couch. He put his feet up on the armrest. If he was going to get fired, he was going to milk the moment for all he could.

The door suddenly opened, and he pulled his feet down, then saw that it was just Callie and put them back up. The secretary silently closed the door and left the two of them alone.

"What are you doing here?" she asked.

"Looks like we're both getting canned, huh? I just wish he'd have left it until Monday. I was really enjoying my weekend."

The truth was he was actually glad to usher Doris out of his house. She was intrusive and odd. He had a sudden flash of her waiting for him when he got home, and it filled him with excitement and dread.

Callie paced back and forth over Weissbaum's plush Oriental rug. She was trying to hide her own nervousness, but it was working on Flint. "I'm sure you were, Valentino."

Flint took a slug of scotch. "Would you stop it with that? You have no idea what I do with my time. The truth is I was actually with a colleague researching a very rare Venetian mask I recently collected."

"Oh, so that's why you smell like chlorinated pool water," she said.

"My colleague is also a swimming enthusiast." He drained the glass.

"You two really don't get along, do you?"

Callie and Flint turned to find Weissbaum emerging from a door hidden in the wall of his office. Both of them gasped at the surprise intrusion and then sheepishly blushed.

"At least you're good with surprises," Weissbaum said, gently shutting the door until it was flush to the wall. With a satisfying click, it became absolutely camouflaged once more.

"So *that's* where you keep your bathroom, Noah," Flint said as he sat upright on the couch.

"No, that would be behind the bookshelf."

Noah sauntered over to the bar and removed a bottle of top shelf gin.

"Callie, may I offer you a drink? Your colleague here has already helped himself."

Callie quietly replied, "I'm alright, Mr. Weissbaum. Thank you, though. You uh, you have a lovely office."

Flint watched her, fascinated. It was strange to see such a strong personality suddenly wilt in front of the powers that be. He wondered if Weissbaum had some dirt on her. Maybe she had a past, after all.

Noah poured the gin into a cocktail shaker and added a touch of vermouth, then just a dash of olive juice. He talked as he shook the cocktail up. "I imagine you're both wondering why you're here. If you have any questions for me, I'm all ears. Please ask away."

Flint internally cringed. Classic Weissbaum. He would always open the floor to the other person. Let them go first. Show their vulnerability, put their foot in their mouth. It allowed him to see what cards the other player was holding under the guise of being warm and polite. Normally Flint was able to restrain himself, sometimes even forcing Weissbaum to go first. That day, he betrayed himself.

"What's she doing here? Is this some mediation thing? 'Cause Noah, look, all due respect, I don't need a headshrinker. It was all just a misunderstanding yesterday."

Weissbaum stopped shaking. He gave Flint a cryptic, curious look. Then he laughed.

"You think I've pulled you two in to reprimand you about your squabbling? On Thursday, my new contract starlet threw a bottle of sherry at her director in front of the whole crew. They'll probably both get promotions next week. Don't flatter yourself." Weissbaum poured his dirty martini into a glass. "Are you sure I can't make you anything, Callie?"

She shook her head in tight, efficient movements. All business.

Weissbaum crossed the room slowly, as if each step carried great intent and gravity. He came to a stop at his desk, a massive thing carved from dark oak. It was covered with books and scripts, along with various headshots, family photos, and award statues. Weissbaum's desk alone contained more achievements than most humans accumulate through an entire life. The studio head turned and leaned against the oak behemoth, taking in the entire room, and setting himself at the head of the metaphorical table. Flint had to hand it to the man, he exuded authority. Weissbaum took a sip of the martini and nodded in approval. He carefully set the glass down and then leaned back against the desk. He looked in silence at Callie, then Flint. Finally, just as the tension was growing too much to bear, he spoke.

"Flint, I am, as you know, and Callie, as you will learn, a student of history. Of culture. Of truth. You see, these are the building blocks that we create films from.

Otherwise, they have no grounding. No intrinsic value. A cowboy picture with no historical honesty is nothing more than mindless entertainment. Now, you ground that cowboy picture realities of human experience or as is too often the case, human tragedy, and you have something worth saving. You have a film that people will remember and return to. It's why Horizon films stay in theaters longer than anyone else's. It's why I've hired both of you. Two very different people, you've both worked hard to maintain that. But two people with unique experiences, with convictions, and with a respect for the truth."

Now that it seemed as if his job was safe, Flint felt more at ease. He rose from the sofa and walked to the bar, where he poured himself a second scotch. He took a sip.

"This is excellent, Noah. Really. What is this flavor? Is that peat?"

"Hm." Noah looked at him with a tired bemusement. He continued, "The funny thing about film and the truth is that it is a double-edged sword. I think we can all agree that all film is a kind of propaganda, yes? That is, no matter what the intention, it is designed to manipulate viewers to a desired feeling. Based upon your conversation with Michael yesterday, I would say that you are both dedicated to using film as propaganda for good. Films that, yes, entertain, but also present a fair portrayal of the human condition. A kind of truth, even as a man is chased through a temple by a giant boulder."

"See, I told you they couldn't have made it that spherical," Flint said.

Callie narrowed her eyes and said, "He's specifically telling us that that's not the point. Right, sir? Am I getting that?"

Noah only smiled at both of them and took a sip of his drink. He cleared his throat and said, "Recently, I was confronted with a different kind of cinematic truth. See, I'm a lucky man. I have friends and family and industry peers all over the world. I hear things before nearly anyone else in this great nation and I get access to new pictures before everyone, anywhere. A couple of weeks ago, a friend of mine in Austria sent me a film that was just released in Germany. Directed by a very talented young woman who, unfortunately, is applying her prodigious ability to a frightening cause. The film is called *The Triumph of the Will.* It's being billed as a documentary, but it's nothing more than bald-faced propaganda for Adolf Hitler and his Nazi party.

"Seeing the nationalism on display, the way these crowds clamor for their leader, it… it frightened me.

"And this is what I mean when I say a double-edged sword. As much as film is capable of reflecting the truth, it is equally adept at distorting it. Or, perhaps more dangerously, *creating* it. The more films that are made, the more moving images become the primary source of entertainment, the more elusive the truth will become. Callie, I can see you're weary of standing, please take a seat by the fire."

Callie nodded in agreement and sat, obviously appreciating the enormous leather chair. Flint spoke up from the bar.

"Noah, I don't mean to rush you, but what does this have to do with us?"

"Apologies, Flint. I got a little off track. I think I made this martini a little stronger than I meant to. The reason I'm talking about the Nazis and their new film is that I have been hearing rumors coming out of Germany for a while now. Media control, the building of a massive army, restrictions on Jews. Some of my own family have become victims of casual antisemitism. I believed these things were happening, but I wanted to remain optimistic. *The Triumph of the Will* told me what I already know. They are going to get much worse."

"I'm so sorry your family is going through that," Callie said. "That's horrible."

Noah nodded, sagely. He drained the last of his martini with a stony, stoic expression.

"Thank you, Callie. I'm already arranging to have them immigrate here where they'll be safe. I intend to pull as many strings as I can and fund as many trips out for Jewish families as I can." For a moment he took in the room as if tallying up the value of all of the paintings and crystal glasses and golden trophies. Then he said, "We must all stand up and do something. Even if we're just filmmakers. We must do what we can. That's where you two come in.

"You see, there's another rumor that I heard. Hitler and his friends are obsessed with the occult. They believe in a dark magick, the kind of old-world worship that is said to have been in Europe for centuries. They are traveling the world trying to uncover what they can. They've even formed a group called the Ahnenerbe. It's a team of academics and archaeologists intent on pillaging the world to find proof of Aryan achievements."

Flint snorted a laugh into his highball glass. The whole thing was so ludicrous sounding.

"This can't be real. It can't be. This is absolutely crazy. The German military hunting for black magick? I mean… Noah. Come on."

"I thought the same thing at first," Weissbaum said. "But you're a student of history, Flint. Think back on everything that man has done to wield power. To destroy other men. Across all races, cultures, creeds. It's the one thing that unites us all, isn't it? Our want to dominate and control. We'll go to the ends of the earth to try and sate that hunger for blood."

Flint realized his boss was right. Global human history was awash with genocide and subjugation. The hunt for magickal relics may have sounded ridiculous at first, but it was rooted in something all too mundanely human.

Flint said, "Okay, I see it. You're right."

"I know I am, Flint. I know."

Weissbaum gave him a rare smile and Flint returned it.

"I've recently received inside information that the Ahnenerbe are planning a secret exploration in North America. A small island off the coast of Nova Scotia called Oak Island. There have long been tales claiming that some of the Knights Templar fled to Oak Island in 1307 to avoid arrest and execution by King Philip the VI. Supposedly the Knights Templar worshipped a strange object-"

Flint interrupted him, "Nuts! No way, Noah. This really is too much."

"What?" Callie asked him. "Weren't the Knights Templar just soldiers for the Catholic church? During the Crusades, right?"

"Exactly, yeah," Flint said, "But then they got too powerful. They wanted to form their own nation state. They became a real pain in the ass to the powers that be. You know the church and what not. They were accused of hoarding spoils of war, which they definitely were. But they were also accused of other indecent things like spitting on the cross, kissing each other-"

"Seriously?" Callie rolled her eyes.

"And worshiping false idols," Weissbaum said.

"Right, that. Amongst those idols was a really, really cuckoo whacky one. The head of John the Baptist."

Now it was Callie's turn to laugh. "What? A severed head?"

"Of the one and only Johnny, best pal of Jesus himself. Supposedly the head could grant worshippers magical powers. Greater intellect, faster reflexes in battle. Immortality, of course. There'd be no point if it didn't make you immortal. Did I miss anything, Noah?"

Weissbaum crossed the room to the bar and began to eyeball the bottles, searching for his next beverage.

"No, you covered it all, Flint." As he perused his bar, Weissbaum said, "Do I believe it? Not likely. Is it possible? Anything is possible. As a proud Jew, I don't believe in the literal power of anything related to a New Testament Christ, but I do understand that, if found, this would be a very powerful- Oh yes, this brandy is excellent- a very powerful tool of propaganda for the Nazi party."

He carefully removed a bottle of cognac and set it aside, then went back to scanning the shelves.

"Flint, do I have any Cointreau?"

"It's up there, top shelf on the left."

Callie mouthed the words *kiss ass* at Flint. He flipped her off.

"Are you making a sidecar, Noah?"

"I am."

"Can I get one?"

"I'll have one as well, if you don't mind," Callie said.

"That's the spirit!" Weissbaum cheered as he pulled down the Cointreau. He began to delicately measure out the ingredients into a fresh cocktail shaker. "Now, here's where you finally come in. I believe that you are a perfect pair to put a stop to this madness in Oak Island. Flint, will you rim these glasses with sugar?"

"Excuse me? Why us?" Callie asked, so shocked that she couldn't help but drop her polite tone.

Weissbaum laughed. "Good question!" He raised his voice to compete with the sound of the ice he was shaking in the cocktail mixer. "Yesterday I saw the two of you team up against one of our most successful directors to try and bring the truth to light. That struck me. You both believe in something bigger. You're both willing to speak truth to power. To risk it for what you think is important. Flint, for you that's the history of the most miraculous of animals: humans. Callie, for you it is the engine that keeps those humans learning and growing: story."

Satisfied with his concoction, Weissbaum poured them out into the three glasses that Flint had added sugar to. Each pour was perfect, not a drop over the line. Weissbaum stepped back and admired his work.

He continued, "I suppose, at the end of the day, I just have a feeling about it down in my gut. And my gut is always right. So that's why it will be the two of you. Flint, you'll be in charge of retrieving and securing the severed head of John the Baptist, should you find it. Callie, you will be there to document the entire experience with camera and pen. There is no use to a story like this if we cannot document it ourselves. Double-edged sword and all that, right? Let's make this edge fall on the side of good."

As Weissbaum spoke, Callie had approached the bar and was now sitting on a stool beside Flint. Flint admired her posture. She had the ability to stand out in whatever space she was in without seeming like she was trying.

"This sounds dangerous. And slightly insane. What's in it for me?" Callie said.

"Ah, there she is!" Weissbaum's eyes sparkled. "Well, how about if you come back from this trip, I get a book and movie deal based on your little adventure? Both of your names, up in lights. More importantly, of course, your truth up on the big screen."

Callie and Flint locked eyes. In that moment, without a word, they both knew what the other was thinking. *Yes.*

"Where do I sign, boss?" Flint asked.

"I'm in too," Callie said.

"Excellent." Weissbaum pushed the glasses across the bar to his two new adventurers. "Let's have this drink be our contract. L'chaim."

Callie and Flint echoed him in unison. "L'chaim."

They all took a sip and let the sweet, sour warmth of the cocktail sink into their bellies. The energy between the three was nervous, but optimistic. Electric and crackling with anticipation.

Suddenly, Weissbaum remembered a detail. "Oh, and you'll be joined by an old friend of mine, Major Jake Roy. We served together in WWI. He's a tough guy. A mercenary."

Callie choked on her drink. "A mercenary?" she spat.

"Don't worry. He's a big lug, as they'd say. A sweet man at heart, but deadly with just about anything you hand him. He's just a precaution. In case the Nazis try to kill you."

CHAPTER 3

Flint poked lazily at his creamed spinach and wondered if the fork was real silver. From what he could tell of their train's first-class dining room, Weissbaum had spared no expense in shuttling his team across the country. Callie sat next to him in their booth, her face pushed up against the glass, watching the world whip by.

The only reason Flint could think would make Callie sit with him was that Maj. Jake Roy occupied the other side of the table. The man was as wide as a Westinghouse refrigerator and at least a head taller. His biceps made Flint feel like a limp piece of spaghetti, and Flint was no slouch in the fitness department. But it was the Major's face that made him really imposing. His stony, angular visage reminded Flint of an Easter Island head, and a black leather eyepatch covered his left eye. The man had barely said two words since they'd left Los Angeles and they were now past Illinois. He didn't seem to eat, either. He just kept drinking mug after mug of earl grey tea, though it was really more sugar squares than tea once he had it the way he liked it.

Who knew an adventurer could be so damn dull? Flint wondered. He sighed and drummed his fingers along the tabletop, working out a slow jazz number, "It Happened in Monterey" by Paul Whiteman and his orchestra. Flint wondered how the orchestra guys felt about being credited that way. He didn't think he'd like it all too well.

"Would you please stop?" Callie asked.

"Sorry, I'm just trying to liven things up a bit. Dinner and show," Flint offered.

"Well then at least pick another song. I really hate that tune."

Flint gave in and quit drumming. He took a bite of his swordfish, swallowed, and said, "Penny for your thoughts, Major."

The man trained his one good eye on Flint and sized him up, unamused. His gaze reminded Flint of a shark he had encountered off the shore of Belize during a post-graduate expedition. He'd had to clock the thing on the nose to keep it from taking a bite out of him. He hoped he wouldn't have to clock Maj. Roy. He didn't think he would be as successful.

Looking around the rich food and richer people populating the dining car, Flint felt a bit embarrassed. He hated to admit it, but he'd grown accustomed to this kind of treatment in Los Angeles. He didn't know if he'd have the wherewithal to punch a shark in the face again and it concerned him. Was he not the adventurer he had once been? Was Callie right? Was he just another Hollywoodland playboy?

As he was examining his own credibility, someone in the sea of snobs caught his eye. It was a man on the opposite side of the car, a few booths down. He was sitting alone and had ordered nothing. Curiously, he'd kept his hat and coat on. He was acting as if he was reading the newspaper, but Flint was positive that he saw him peering over the top of the paper to study them. For a split second he locked eyes with Flint and immediately went back to his paper. A waiter came by for his order and the man moved him along.

"I wonder if they have any more deviled eggs," Roy said.

Both Callie and Flint turned to him, shocked that he would volunteer to speak.

"What?" Callie asked.

“Flint asked what was on my mind. I just told you.”

Flint said, “Looking around at this place I bet they would make another plate just for you if you asked really sweetly.”

Roy grunted. “I will go to the kitchen and ask.”

He got up and as he walked past, Flint grabbed him by the sleeve of his unseasonable wool blazer. The look Roy gave him made him regret it.

Flint swallowed and said, “I was just going to add, uh, see if you can get a few oysters Rockefeller. I wouldn’t mind that.”

Roy grunted again and moved away down the train car. Flint watched as the wait staff navigated around the man who pressed onward through any social obstacle like the train itself.

“Well, now we can enjoy the countryside together,” Flint said.

Callie didn’t reply.

He continued, hoping to at least annoy her into a response, “Look at that beautiful countryside out there. Idyllic. Bucolic, really. Farmers and hay and cows and… hay. We get all up our own keester’s out in Los Angeles, but this here, this is the real America. These rural United States, that’s heaven.”

She whirled on him and snapped, “Why are you incapable of handling even a minute of silence? What is wrong with your brain?” Then she took a breath and said, softer, “I’m sorry. I just…if you’ve actually lived out there you would know that it’s really not that great.”

“Jesus, okay. I’ll leave you alone.”

Flint wasn’t that hungry, short of a craving for oysters Rockefeller, but he tried to turn his attention back to his swordfish. Still, he couldn’t shake the feeling that he was being watched. The same creeping dread that he’d had when he found Weissbaum eyeballing him on set just a few days prior. And that had turned out swimmingly. He looked up at the Newspaper Man and caught him peering over the paper. Again, he acted like he'd been caught and turned back to the paper. The fellow wasn't even trying to be subtle. Flint got a knot in the pit of his stomach. The guy was bad news.

He leaned over to Callie and said, "I'm not trying to annoy you right now, this is a serious question. What's your read on that guy?"

Callie considered it and said, "Well, he's odd. But he's plenty rugged. The strong, silent type I guess. The eyepatch is a bit…haunting."

A weird feeling flashed in Flint. Jealousy. *No, it couldn't be.* He pushed it down. He said, "Not Roy, dingbat. That guy."

He tried to jerk his thumb in a subtle way toward the man in the hat and coat. Callie followed and checked the man out.

"Oh. Hm. Who wears a hat at dinner? He's odd too."

"I think he's been watching us."

"Seriously? Is there a spy in our midst?" Her eyes went wide with faux shock and her tone was full of sarcastic enthusiasm.

"Yes, seriously. I'm not playing around. I made eye contact with him, and he looked really spooked."

"I'm sure he's just drawn to your natural charm, Flint." Callie reached over with her fork and took a bite of Flint's creamed spinach. "Ugh, this is a little cold. It's all gluey."

"Dammit, I'm telling you- Try some pepper on it, it livens it up a bit- I'm telling you there's something hinky with that guy. Listen, I'm going to get up and go to the bathroom. I want to see if he follows me. Stay here and don't tell the Major what I'm doing. I don't want him unleashing the Hundred Days Offensive all over the train. At least not yet."

Callie rolled her eyes as she sprinkled pepper on the spinach. "I think I can handle that, pally."

"Wonderful. Oh, and couple oysters for me."

Flint walked by the Newspaper Man, but deliberately kept his eyes up. He pushed the heavy metal door at the end of the train car and stepped outside, letting it fall behind him. The train tracks whizzed by beneath his feet. Wind whipped around him. Railings extended to the end of each train car and were connected by loose chains. He gripped the railings as he stepped from one car to the next. He definitely wasn't the adventurer he once was, he thought sadly. Weissbaum had no idea he was sending a man who needed handrails out into the field.

As he went to open the door into the next train car, a reflection caught his eye in the glass window. Back in the first-class dining car, the Newspaper Man was moving up from his booth and coming his way. Flint quickly pulled the door open and moved into the next car containing the second-class dining area.

Right as he stepped in, a harried waiter bumped into him with a tray of coffee mugs. A bit splashed on Flint's suit lapel.

"Oh, uh, I'm terribly sorry, sir. It's just so busy and I-"

"Not a problem," Flint said and meant it. "Where's the bathroom?"

"You've actually just passed it. It's on the entrance door by your left. And thank you, sir."

"Don't mention it."

He turned back the way he'd come and caught a glimpse of the Newspaper Man crossing between the cars. He slipped into the bathroom as quickly as he could and locked the door behind him.

He turned the faucet on and splashed some cold water on his face. Something was definitely up. There was no way the stranger's movements were a coincidence at this point. *What was the guy's end goal?* Flint wondered. *Who knows? Maybe he'll be gone.*

Flint took a deep breath and opened the door. The man was not gone. In fact, he was standing right in front of the door with a switchblade in his hand.

"Please, you are coming vith me now," the man said in a thick German accent.

"So, the Reich's not giving their thugs English lessons anymore, huh?"

For the first time he got a good look at the man's face. A little upturned pug nose, narrow eyes, tightly cropped blonde hair peeking out from under the hat. Despite a pencil-thin neck he had a jowly, bloated face. Flint wanted to give him a little pig snort and shout "Sooooo-wee!" in his face, but he wasn't the one with the knife.

"Vat?" the man asked him.

"While I appreciate your negotiation tactic here, the knife and all that, I'm not going anywhere with you."

Flint eyeballed his escape options. To his right was the first-class dining car. It seemed the smartest option given that there was a mercenary hired to deal with exactly such an occurrence. Unfortunately, Newspaper Man had angled himself to strategically block that pathway. It would have to be the other way, through the second-class dining car and beyond.

"Go now!" the thug hissed.

Flint juked to the right, making him think he was trying to wriggle past and making the man jump to cover the exit. Then, Flint took off to the left through the second-class dining car, buying himself a few seconds as the guy staggered against the wall and then took off after him.

Flint sprinted around free-standing tables and shocked diners. He could hear the man's feet pounding behind him and knew he wasn't far behind. As he neared the end of the car he ran toward one of the booths lining the side walls of the car.

"I'm so sorry for this," he said to the family of four enjoying their dinner.

He then grabbed their tablecloth and jerked it, pulling the entire tabletop down to the floor. As he pulled the exit door open he looked back for a split second. Newspaper Man was down on the floor, covered in Salisbury steak gravy and cursing in German.

Flint smirked and kept running. He leapt between the two cars and swung the door open with ease. No second thoughts. It reminded him of the time he had been chased out of a yurt bar by a very angry Mongolian who then tracked him over several miles. He'd finally outrun the guy and didn't get the pummeling he probably deserved for making fun of his mother over a hand of cards.

He continued on into the entertainment car, where a jazz trio was striking up a fun rhythm. All around him, couples were doing the Lindy hop and the jitterbug. He darted around them like a football receiver sprinting through the defensive line. He had no idea where the Newspaper Man was at this point, but he assumed he was still hot on his trail.

Suddenly he was confronted with a dancing couple right in the middle of a big swing move. There was no way anyone could get out of the way in time. Flint knew that if he bumped into them, he was caught. Just as the man was rolling his girl over his back, Flint dropped to the ground and slid across the slick dance floor, right between the man's legs, like Akry Vaughan sliding into home.

Flint passed through the startled couple, scrambled to his feet, and kept moving. It was then that a sign near the exit caught his eye. It said, "To Kitchen," with an arrow pointing to the left. Right before he hit the door connecting the two trains he took a tight left and found himself at the bottom of a narrow flight of stairs. Without the time to consider it, he sprinted up the stairwell.

As he turned a tight corner he bumped into someone; the waiter who'd spilled the coffee on him just moments before. He tried to move around the man, who was now struggling with a tray of steaming cups of turtle soup. The stairs were too cramped, and he accidentally knocked the man down.

"Are you serious?!" the man called out as he tumbled down the stairs, spilling soup everywhere.

"Apologies, buddy! I'll tip you later!"

Flint sped through the swinging door into the kitchen and was suddenly confronted with total chaos. Smoke and fire, steam and screaming. Between the wait staff grabbing meals and the chefs preparing them, there was so much activity that no one seemed to notice Flint as he ran along a counter, grabbing a meat cleaver and an iron skillet.

They definitely noticed when he stopped in the middle of the kitchen and whirled around, brandishing the pan and the cleaver like a gladiator in the middle of the ring. The work stopped and a hush fell across the kitchen. Newspaper Man stood in the doorway, red faced and furious, covered in sauces and soup. The switchblade was clutched in his fist.

"Why are you after me?" Flint asked.

The man spoke in between ragged breaths. "I been with you since you have left Los Angeles. I know that you vill try to stop our progress. That must not be allowed."

"What are you gonna do about it, bud?"

"Of course, I vill take your life on behalf of mein Führer."

"Yeah, of course," Flint muttered. He spoke to the kitchen staff, who all remained frozen at their stations. "You all might want to go catch a flick or something. It's about to get a little unsafe in here."

As they all sprang into action and hurried out the door behind the Newspaper Man, Flint squared his shoulders and prepared for battle. It reminded him of the time in India when he fought off a spitting cobra with nothing but a haandi serving bowl. *Surely I can handle one little pig faced Nazi,* he thought.

Just in case, he looked for an alternate exit. The only one he could find was a smoke vent in the ceiling above him. The last of the evening's light shone through. It looked easy enough to punch through and climb up on top of the train. Not ideal, but easy enough.

The Newspaper Man rushed him. The switchblade glinted from the open stove flames around them. *I'm in hell*, Flint thought as the Nazi slashed at him. He deflected the blade with the skillet and then swung at the guy with his cleaver.

His attacker ducked, narrowly avoiding a cleaver to the neck. While he was down, he stabbed the switchblade at Flint's leg. The blade cut through his pant leg and slashed his skin. Flint felt the stinging pain and then the warmth of blood running down his calf.

"Dammit, this suit is Burberry, you jackass!" Flint yelled.

Enraged, he swung aggressively with the meat cleaver and caught flesh. The cleaver dug deeply into the man's bicep, so deeply that it stayed put when Flint let go of the blade and stepped back, taking in the scene with wide-eyed shock. For a second, both men were stunned in speechlessness.

"Oh gee, guy, I- I've never stabbed anyone. Let's just call this and get you a doc-"

Then the Nazi was howling in pain and anger. The Newspaper Man pulled the cleaver from his arm and watched the blood pour from his arm. He looked at Flint with wild eyes. Then he grinned. Obviously, he had no intention of calling the fight.

"Fuck," Flint said.

He leapt up toward the ceiling filter and, using the iron skillet, knocked the metal filter out. The edge of the filter was caught by the air flowing around the speeding train and ripped out. The hole was free.

Flint stuffed the skillet down the front of his slacks, jumped upward, and caught the edges of the hole. He easily lifted himself up and felt the wind against his face. The last thing he thought before he climbed up on top of the train was, *"This is a terrible idea."*

He did it anyway.

He crawled out of the hole and tried to get his bearings. It was nearly dark out. The sun was small on the horizon, lending its last light to the fight of Flint's life. A bridge was coming up, going over a wide river. Flint shrugged. Worst case, he could just jump.

Then he realized that he had the high ground. If the Newspaper Man dared to come up with him, and it seemed pretty likely he would, Flint could probably clock him with the skillet before he realized what was happening.

Flint got to his feet, careful to not fall and slide off the train's roof into oblivion. He crouched, positioning himself near the hole. Sure enough, a moment later the Newspaper Man lifted himself up out of the hole. Flint swung hard and connected with the back of his head. He heard a crunching sound and winced on behalf of the guy.

The man went slack, dropping his switchblade. Before he fell back through the hole, Flint grabbed him around the shoulders and pulled him up on top of the train. The wind caught the man's hat and blew it away, giving Flint a look at the damage he'd caused. The Nazi's head was bleeding badly and there appeared to be a little divot in his skull.

He dropped the Newspaper Man onto the roof and knelt on top of him. The Newspaper Man was dazed, disoriented. Flint slapped him across the face until the man was able to focus on him.

"Who sent you after us? What do they know?"

The man managed to smile at him, the same creepy grin he'd given him after he'd pulled a meat cleaver out of his own arm.

"I know nothing," he said.

"Who's leading the research team? I want names, damn you! What do they have waiting for us?"

"I know nothing," he said again.

Flint stood up and grabbed the man by the lapels. He yanked him upward until the man was standing unsteadily on his own feet. They both nearly fell over when the train lurched as it transitioned onto the bridge. Endless blue water spread out on either side of the two men.

"So, I'm not getting anything, is that what you're telling me?" Flint asked.

"I…I know…"

"Yeah, yeah, nothing. I get it."

Flint dragged the man to the very edge of the train.

"When you wash up on shore, tell Hitler I said to suck a knockwurst, will you?"

With that, Flint flung the man over the side of the train. He listened to the Nazi's screams. He watched as he landed in the water below. He grinned to himself as the man struggled in the water, angrily flapping his arms like a cat in a bathtub.

Flint turned to face the direction the train was moving in and watched the world race toward him. The wind rustled his hair, and the sunset touched his face and felt like he was riding a savage beast into a strange new future. Perhaps he wasn't so far away from the man who had had all of those experiences abroad. Perhaps he was still an adventurer after all. He smiled.

CHAPTER 4

"It's actually kind of beautiful," Callie said, gazing out the window of the little seaplane that was carrying them to Oak Island. "Not sure what I was expecting."

Roy grunted in agreement. He said, "Never thought I'd say this, but Canada might be as pretty as Michigan."

"You from Michigan, then?" Flint asked, thinking he had finally learned something about the soldier and desperate to make conversation.

"Huh? No," Roy said.

"Oh. Great."

Flint had tried to hide it but being on the tiny plane was rattling him. The tight cabin was bringing up feelings of claustrophobia, a panic inducing fear that had gripped him ever since the boyhood day he'd fallen into the tightly compacted bowels of the pyramid. He'd been white knuckling it since they'd flown out of Bangor and made their way into Nova Scotia. Talking helped him keep the fear at bay, but his companions were of little help.

To keep his mind occupied, he looked out the window at their destination. It was indeed beautiful. A small island full of lush, emerald forest. It reminded him that the world didn't look like Los Angeles, and he was surprised at his own gratitude for that.

"Nice to be out of LA." He forced a laugh. "Really, I'm just glad to be off of that train. I was going stir crazy."

Callie didn't look away from the window. "You made the crazy part perfectly clear. I cannot imagine how much Weissbaum must have wired those cops that met us at the Cleveland station to let you go. I mean, you nearly killed a guy in their kitchen."

"First of all, he nearly killed me. I got three stitches in my leg, and he ruined those Burberry pants. *Ruined.* Secondly, he wasn't a 'guy,' he was a Nazi spy who wanted to kill us."

Flint put air quotes around 'guy' and Callie rolled her eyes.

"Don't air quote to me, Mr. McQuaid. That is extremely irritating."

"Why don't we all just keep our yappers shut?" Roy grumbled. His voice sounded like gravel churning around in a cement mixer.

"Yeah, sure, great idea. Thanks, Roy," Flint said.

"I'm supposed to tell you we're beginning our descent," the pilot said laconically. "So, we're beginning our descent."

Flint white knuckled the arm rests on his chair until the plane finally touched down in a cove at the east end of the island. It hit the water with a little shake, its pontoons cutting through the sea. Then, a sudden jolt. The shrieking of metal. Everyone flew forward in the cabin, banging their heads and limbs.

"Ow! Dammit!" Flint cried out.

The pilot looked back from his seat and said, "I'm awfully sorry, I have no idea what that was."

He gunned the plane's engine, but it wouldn't move.

"We're definitely stuck," he said. "Anyone want to go out and take a look?"

"You're the plane expert," Flint said.

"Oh for- I'll check it out!" Callie opened the door to the plane and, without hesitation, leapt down into the water.

Roy and Flint exchanged a look and then followed, quickly finding themselves waist deep in chilly Canadian sea water. Callie was already over by the left pontoon, which had been decimated by a large rock in the water. The metal was twisted up and broken open, allowing water to slosh into the pontoon itself.

"Looks like we found the culprit," Callie said.

"Hell's bells!" the pilot shouted from his open side window. "That's gonna be a problem."

"No kidding," Flint quipped.

"Not helpful," Callie said.

The pilot continued, "That water coming in is gonna have this baby sinking in the next fifteen minutes or so. We need some guys out here to get this thing unstuck so I can bob into shore."

"I don't suppose you can take off like this?" Flint asked.

"Oh no, there's no flying outta here 'til I can find a specialist. Let's hope this is the kind of island that serves mai tais."

"I seriously doubt it."

Roy was already working on pushing the pontoon off of the rock. His thick, corded muscles bulged beneath his safari shirt and his face flushed a bright red. Flint was worried he might have a heart attack right there in the water. He moved to help, but the Major waved him away.

Instead, Flint examined the rock itself. It was curved outward and upward, coming to a point at the end, like a talon. He'd never seen a rock naturally shaped like that. It had to have been hand carved. It was high tide, and the sharp end of the rock came to just below the surface. High enough to cause damage to any vessel trying to enter the little cove, but low enough that it wouldn't be seen.

"Look at this," Flint said to Roy. "This thing is a trap. It has to be."

"And we went right into it. Now we have to get out."

Fair enough, Flint thought. *No use crying over spilt milk. Or learning anything from it either, apparently.* Flint said none of this. Roy was actually making some headway with the pontoon, and he didn't want the enormous man to spend all of his strength punching him in the face.

It wasn't that he didn't think he could do some damage to Roy. Hell, he'd just thrown a Nazi off of a moving train. He would definitely give Roy a run for his money. But he was pretty sure that the man who was nearly twice his size and trained by the world's most shadowy military programs would end up besting him no matter what. Besides, Flint hadn't seen enough to trust the guy yet and didn't know what he was capable of. He seemed like the kind to go off half-cocked and keep punching well after the fight was done.

Flint looked around for Callie. She was already halfway to land. She was standing in water up to her knees and peering down at the water as if it held the secrets to crafting her next hit movie script. Flint slogged his way through the water to her.

"That rock is a trap," he said. "Hard carved."

Callie looked up, and arched an eyebrow with genuine interest. *Finally, someone who cares*!

"No kidding?" Callie asked.

"No kidding."

"I've got something whacky here too…" She pointed at the water immediately below her. "What does that look like to you?"

The water was murky, but Flint could see the outline of something on the cove floor. Two thick, open pipes, about four inches in diameter each, ran from their feet and toward the land. The pipe disappeared under sand a few beyond them so there was no way of telling where it was actually headed.

"Some sort of irrigation system?" Callie asked.

"It looks like it," Flint said.

He knelt down in the water and reached beneath the surface, running his hands along the exposed pipes.

"These are old. Roughhewn… The interior texture… it feels like it wasn't created using a vitrification process…"

Callie didn't kneel down into the water with him. "How old?"

"At least five hundred years, I would say."

"Your clothes are soaked, you look silly," Callie said. "But this is good. What else?"

"Well, it feels like terra cotta, which is very strange because terra cotta was used by the Chinese and the Greeks. Sometimes Mesopotamians in their sculpture work-"

"Oh God, you're even more boring when you're an egghead. Get to the point."

Flint stood up and tried to shake the water off of his arms before deciding it was a futile gesture.

"The point, my dear Callie, is the natives of this island, whoever they may have been, wouldn't have created pipes like this."

"So, five hundred years ago-"

"At *least* five hundred years ago," Flint interrupted.

"-before Columbus, someone from Europe or China came to this island."

Flint didn't know what to say. When she laid it out like that it sounded insane. Besides, they hadn't even gotten on the island yet and he was already drawing conclusions that would have upended the last few centuries of recorded Western history.

"Well, I don't know, I- I suppose so. *Possibly*."

Callie looked inland, to the thick forest beyond the shallow, sandy shoreline. To her, the forest looked impenetrable. Shadowy. Mysterious, but not with the promise of treasure. With the promise of something much, much darker.

"There's something about this place. Something strange. Something a bit sinister…"

Flint followed her gaze, tried to see the island the way she saw it. He couldn't deny that there was something there that gave him an unsettling little tingle up his spine. He didn't want to say anything to make her more troubled. He'd learned by experience that strange, untouched historical places could bring on a feeling one might academically call the 'heebie jeebies.' Before he could answer they heard Roy call out from behind them.

"A little help here?! We need to hide this big bastard in those trees along the shoreline!"

They turned to find that Roy had tied a large length of rope from one tripod stilt to the next. He and the pilot, who looked absolutely heartbroken to be out of his seat, were set up like plow horses ready to pull the plane in. Roy pointed to a thick cropping of sumac trees that, along with the help of some friendly shrubbery, would hide the plane from prying eyes.

"We're going to drag a plane?" Flint said, quietly enough that Roy couldn't hear.

Callie snorted a laugh and punched him in the shoulder.

"Saddle up, pally. Let's go."

He watched her tall, well-built frame move through the water and hated that he enjoyed watching how she moved. It wasn't even from a physical standpoint, at least not completely. It was how she navigated the world. It intrigued him in a way that he couldn't put his finger on.

"Wake up, McQuaid. Quit daydreaming and help us get this damn plane in!" Roy shouted.

***

At the top of a hill overlooking the cove, hiding between the yellow birches, a man watched them. A young German soldier, in fact. He lowered his binoculars and grinned as the man they called Flint struggled to get the pulling rope in place. He would have laughed but had been warned against such gaiety by his superiors.

"How are they faring down there?" he heard a voice speak in German behind him.

Startled, he dropped the binoculars. He hoped that it wasn't Sauer coming up on him. The man gave him the creeps, the way he was constantly hovering, silently criticizing all the soldiers on the Ahnenerbe crew. Sauer would only claim that he was a scientist, an expert on the Aryan race and their genetic superiority. But his fellow soldiers claimed there were rumors about him. Dark rumors about what he did behind locked laboratory doors. Sauer's silence about his work only increased the rumors.

The young soldier was relieved to see it was just the archaeologist.

"Hello, soldier. Baldur, right?"

"Obersoldat Baldur Axmann, sir."

Obersoldat. Just a private. The archaeologist picked up the binoculars and handed them to the soldier with a smile. He looked out at the cove below them. At the four people struggling to pull the barely floating plane behind them like pack mules. He watched Flint and snickered to himself.

"He's funny, that one," he said, pointing at Flint.

The soldier allowed himself to smile. He said, "Yes, he is."

To the kid he said, "Is this what you thought you'd be doing when you joined up with the SS?"

The kid looked at the ground, bashful. "I never thought about any of this. I wanted to be a runner. Track and field. Olympics and all. Then the war, and- Well, my father is a… this is embarrassing. My father is a high ranking official in the SS. He had me assigned."

The archaeologist laid a hand on his shoulder. He spoke with a warmth that surprised the boy. The man seemed so genuine. That was rare in difficult times, and the boy appreciated it.

The archaeologist said, "Don't be embarrassed by that. My father helped me. He's why I'm here. The more I've seen of the world, and I've seen quite a bit I think, the more I believe that all men just want to be their fathers. We fight it like hell when we're boys, but boys become men. And men are gifted a destiny when they take that last name. I'm sorry, I don't mean to lecture you."

"No, no, it's good. Maybe you're right," the boy said thoughtfully.

"Just remember that sometimes the easy path only seems easy because it's natural. You can't spend your whole life fighting."

"Should I report their arrival?" the kid asked.

"I'm not your superior," the archaeologist replied. "I don't know all that military procedure, Baldur."

"Right, of course. That was silly."

"But yes, I would report their arrival immediately if I were you."

The archaeologist looked out over the water and the group was gone. Vanished. That pleased him. It would take some work to track them down. They might even beat them to the artifact, an idea that also gave the man a jolt of excitement.

Then he said quietly, to himself, "Actually, it's funny. I look forward to seeing him again. I didn't expect that."

The kid sensed that the man was having a moment and needed some privacy. Besides, his job was done.

"Well, I'll go tell them, Dr. McQuaid."

"Oh please, no military procedure! Call me Declan."

CHAPTER 5

A wind rustled the leaves of the birch trees and sent a chill running through Callie. She hugged her thick wool sweater tighter around her. The sweater had been her father's, and while it had dwarfed her when she was a girl, it now fit her almost as well as it had fit him. She was only an inch shorter than he had been. The sweater reminded her of the best times of her childhood. The worst times, too. Those seemed to overshadow the good. She pushed the memories from her mind and tried to stay focused on the present.

The camp had sprung up around them in a matter of a couple of hours, all built by a handful of locals that Weissbaum had employed from afar to follow Maj. Roy's every command. He'd barely spoken to the men, but he hadn't needed to. They were rough, callused men. Former soldiers and current loggers. Builders of homes and breakers of horses. They knew what to do and fell in line. She was glad to have them there.

She smiled to herself as she watched Flint stand up on a chair and clink a fork against a tin cup. *Ting, ting, ting*. The men, some drinking beer, some eating, some dozing by the fire, looked up one by one. Their faces were a mix of apathy, confusion, annoyance. Who was this man with his perfect mustache and fine suit? Roy looked up and then went back to cleaning a revolver that he had partially disassembled in his lap.

Flint cleared his throat. "As the leader of this group of merry researchers, I wanted to say something tonight. First, I want to thank you for joining us Americans on this adventure. I can't say that it will be easy. I can't say that it will be safe. But I can say that we should all end up a good deal richer than we are today. We may also be making discoveries that could change our understanding of human history. At the very least Canadian history, right?"

"Same thing," one of the men quipped.

Flint laughed along with the group. "I think you're righter than you know, sir!"

The men nodded along. A couple even clapped. Callie had to admit it: Flint had a motormouth on him, but he could win people over. She didn't admire that, necessarily. It was representative of a salesman-like quality that made her bristle. She did, however, envy it. Life was easier for people like Flint. *Men* like Flint more specifically. So many of her conversations seemed to turn into arguments. Maybe that was because that was all she'd seen when she was young.

The cold wind hit her again, sharper this time. She shivered. The trees that towered around her seemed menacing. She hadn't been able to shake the same uneasy feeling that had hit her when she'd first headed toward the shore that day. She wondered if this whole thing had been a bad idea. All the movie deals in the world wouldn't mean a thing if she was strung up from a pine and left swinging in the cold wind by a Nazi or a ghost or a rabid bear or whatever else was inhabiting the thick woods around them.

She jumped as she felt something pull against her leg. A scream caught in her throat.

"Miss?"

She looked down to find a little girl tugging on her pants. Callie wasn't much for gauging the ages of kids, but the girl didn't come up much higher than her waist. She wore a dress with her stockings pulled up and an old wool coat that hit a bit too high above her wrists. She was thin, her cheeks sunken.

"Oh, uh, hi kiddo." Callie was still jittery from the surprise and the words caught in her throat.

"My name is Shirley," the girl said softly.

Callie knelt down and whispered to the girl, not wanting to bring undue attention from Flint's speech. The girl seemed to have something important, perhaps even secret, to tell her. Besides, she assumed one of the men was Shirley's father and didn't want to risk his getting mad at her for interrupting. She knew what it was like to be a girl on the receiving end of that kind of frustration.

"Hi, Shirley. I'm Callie. I like your name."

The girl blushed.

"Is one of these men your daddy?"

She shook her head. "I don't got a daddy. I mean, I did, but he's gone. He went away. I heard you needed people to work for you. To help out. I can do a lot of things."

"I know you can, Shirley."

"My mama needs help. For food and things, you know?"

"I do know. I know exactly what you mean."

"What if I could tell you something I bet is real important for you to know? Would that be a job? A job for money?"

"Of course. That would be the most important job."

Shirley looked around like a spy making sure the coast was clear. Callie played along.

"Those men from Europe-"

"The Germans? The ones in black uniforms?" Callie clarified.

"Yeah, them ones. I seen where they're digging around, looking for treasures. They're digging in a place we call the Money Pit."

"Well, that seems like a good place to start."

Shirley didn't seem to find the humor in that.

"Is that good? I can spy more."

"That was very, very good, Shirley. Very good."

Callie reached into her pocket and pulled out a two-dollar bill.

"You can exchange American money, right?"

The girl's hungry eyes lit up, telling her the answer. Callie could tell she was doing all she could to not grab for it. She handed it to Shirley, who politely folded it up and tucked it carefully inside the recesses of her worn coat.

"You come back later and I'll give you more, I promise."

The girl grinned broadly and nodded. Excitedly, she said, "I'll get more information too! I'll follow them all around the island!"

"Those men aren't nice. Don't follow them around. You don't need to do that. I'll still pay you."

"Gotta work to get paid," the girl said. "I'll follow those fellows everywhere. I'm good at hiding!"

The girl flashed her a grin and took off running into the woods, kicking her knobby knees up high. Callie watched her go with a sad smile and hoped against hope that the girl would keep herself safe. When she looked back to Flint, he was finishing up his speech.

"-and so, we'll work together, we'll dig together, and we'll get rich together! Thank you, boys!"

The men clapped. As he stepped down from the chair, he caught her eye and sauntered over to meet her at the outskirts of the camp.

"What're you doing skulking about in the dark, screenwriter? Actually, that's exactly what writers do, isn't it?"

"Shut up, Flint. I've accomplished more out here than you did in your whole hour-long speech."

"I'm a leader of men, what can I say?"

Callie rolled her eyes and shivered against the cold.

Flint said, "There has to be a place to get a drink on this island, right? Warm up a bit?"

Callie arched an eyebrow at him. Said nothing. She pulled her lips so tight the color went out of them.

"Jeez Louise, lighten up, would you? I'm going to try anything. We're coworkers and I'm a gentleman. Also, I'm not interested in you."

Callie considered it. It would be nice to get out of the damn woods and they did need to start putting together a game plan. Alcohol would make Flint a bit more tolerable to deal with, too. Finally, she nodded.

He pumped his fist in the air. "Hallelujah! That's the spirit! Let's go find a little speakeasy around here. Oh wait, did they end prohibition in Canada?"

"Let's hope to God they did," Callie muttered.

***

Flint sat down across from Callie with a pint of nameless beer and a shot glass full of Hermitage whiskey balanced in each hand. Bottled in bond. The old wooden chair creaked under his weight. He looked around the bar. It was an old clapboard box, teetering on the edge of "functioning bar" and "abandoned shack." Everything in it creaked. It was a surprisingly popular spot, full of fishermen and trappers and just plain old shitkicker drunks, all looking for an excuse to get rowdy.

"You're the only dame in here, it appears," Flint said.

Callie ignored him. "I didn't take you for a shot and a beer type," she said.

"Oh, I'm not. I asked for a couple of brown derbies and the guy just stared at me. So, this is what we ended up with. These Canucks, they're straight shooters though, I'll give 'em that. It's not a clip joint."

Callie slammed the shot back and took a long pull from her beer.

"Mmm, room temperature beer. Love it," she said.

"Uh, cheers, then," Flint muttered.

"Sorry, I just need to take the edge off *now*. This island gives me a weird feeling. A dark feeling, you know? Down in my bones."

Just then, a man staggered into their table, jostling the beers. Flint looked up angrily to find a squat, slight little bald man. His eyes were hidden behind circular glasses with smokey, opaque lenses. His hair was so blonde it was almost white. It was cut high and tight on the sides with the top perfectly parted and combed. He stepped back from the table and flapped his long, black leather trench coat.

"Pardon me," he said in a thick, German accent.

His lips were smiling, but his voice was cold and flat.

Flint stood up and said, "Yeah, pally. Pardon you. Maybe you've had one too many belts. Head on home, eh?"

"Yes, perhaps. Too many belts." His lips remained frozen in the strange smile. "I stumbled putting on my coat."

He opened the coat as if to show it off. He revealed a 9mm Luger pistol strapped to his hip. His creepy smile dropped.

"Good night, then," he said, then turned and left.

Flint watched him go out the door before speaking.

"That fellow wasn't at all threatening."

Callie looked around, nervously. "I didn't think this through before I agreed to it. Is it smart for us to be in here? Don't answer that because I know the answer. It's not smart. Do you think he knew who we are?"

"If he knew we were his competition he would have used that little heater to fill us with daylight."

"All I'll say is, I have a bad feeling about this whole place."

"Oh, come on. There's nothing supernatural going on…" Flint didn't want to admit it, but he had been feeling a bit uneasy too since they'd arrived.

"There's something strange going on, on this island. And I don't just mean the Nazis."

She was right. He didn't want to admit that, either. He wanted to have fun. He pounded his shot and took a gulp of beer.

"God, that is warm, huh? You got the map? Let's be constructive with our happy hour."

Callie looked around, cautiously. She reached into a canvas satchel at her feet and pulled out a rolled-up piece of paper. Delicately, she unrolled the paper over the top of the table, displaying a map of the island. She threw one arm around it to hide their work from prying eyes and Flint did the same.

Callie jabbed her finger down at a point on the map. It was situated to the eastern side of the island, not far from the cove they had flow into.

"The Money Pit," Flint said.

"That's right. I got some inside information from a local tonight. The Nazis have started there."

"Smart. The Money Pit is the heart of the whole Oak Island mystery. It's a seemingly endless, cylindrical pit with different levels built into it using logs."

"Sounds like a reverse Empire State Building."

Flint snickered. "Yeah, something like that. The logs were sealed up with putty and coconut fiber. You know what doesn't grow in Novia Scotia? Coconut fiber. But the real shocker was the stone tablet. Eighty-eight feet down, they found this stone that isn't native to the area either. It was carved with these Nordic runes. Translated, it said, 'Forty feet below, two million pounds are buried.'"

Callie choked on her beer.

"Are you kidding me, McQuaid? So, what happened? You keep digging at that point!"

"The tunnel flooded. The treasure hunters almost died. Nobody ever dared to go back in the pit. Until now."

"If anyone has the technology to irrigate the pit, it's the Nazis," Callie said. Then, "Just to be clear here, we're talking about two million British pounds?"

"Or two million pounds of horse shit."

Callie rolled the map back up into a perfectly tight tube and slipped it back into her bag.

She said, "You don't believe it?"

"Who knows? I've learned over the years that belief doesn't have anything to do with it. The world moves around you and makes choices for you. It presents the reality that it's created and leaves you to react to it. One day you're swimming in your pool with two beautiful ladies, the next you're betrayed and trapped in the guts of a pyramid, hoping to not die."

He realized that the shot of whiskey had hit him a little harder than he'd thought, and he was rambling. He clammed up.

"What? That was an oddly specific set of scenarios, Flint."

"My point is… What's my point?" Flint thoughtfully stroked his pencil mustache. Then his eyes lit up. "My point is, I'm pretty open minded about all this and I think you should be too. *But* I also listen to my gut. And my gut tells me that if you had buried two million golden coins on a Canadian island, you wouldn't have put it in a pit out in the open, with a sign telling you exactly where to get it.

"I have my own idea of where we can start tomorrow. But the thing is, Callie. The Germans, they're going to catch wind of us eventually, no matter where we dig."

Callie knew he was right. It worried her. If the weirdo in the black leather coat had been any indication, the Ahnenerbe didn't seem to mind solving things with violence and intimidation. The thought of a real conflict with them made her nervous, but it also made her excited. Every adventure movie needed a little action, and Noah had promised her a film of her own.

"I wouldn't worry too much though." Flint downed the last of his beer and continued. "Not yet, anyway. These things happen at normal dig sites all the time. A rival school or nation or company interest is going after the same bone you are. It ends up being a bunch of academics digging in separate holes twenty feet from each other and exchanging glares. Still, we ought to use the surprise to our advantage. I'm sure they'll try to do something to sabotage us. Might as well use the time we have. Speaking of this local source you've got… think they could do a little spying at the Money Pit for us?"

Callie thought about Shirley, her skinny legs, and hungry eyes, and hoped that wherever she was, she was safe and warm.

"I think we should put Roy on that one," she answered.

Flint nodded. "Smart."

"Or me. I'm not scared of these Nazi thugs," Callie said and an image of Katherine Hepburn saying the same thing on a giant screen flashed in her mind.

"I knew you were a bare-knuckle brawler," Flint said with a grin. "What is this magic? It's… it's somehow empty!"

He picked up and examined Callie's empty beer glass. He let out a theatrical gasp of shock and she snorted a little laugh.

"I just made you laugh! I'm going to get us another round, but before I do I wanted to say that for the last half an hour in this bar, you haven't called me a womanizer or an idiot or a bore."

As he turned to go to the bar, a face emerged out of the crowd. A familiar face to Flint.

Callie watched as Flint stood, walked over to the man whose face betrayed a quick flicker of recognition, and, without a word, hauled back and punched the man in the face. The hit dropped him like a sack of potatoes to the floor of the bar. He was out cold.

Some of the shitkickers stared. Some laughed. Some cheered. None stood up for the man who'd been decked. Flint wasn't the kind of rowdy they were looking for.

Flint left the man lying on the floor. He marched past Callie and moved on toward the door.

Callie called out to his back, "Who in the hell was that?!"

"My brother!" he called back gruffly. As he stepped through the door he added, "He's working for the sons of bitches!"

She looked back to find some locals helping the man up from the floor. He was coming to. He looked at her and smiled. Even though there was blood between his teeth, she recognized the grin as being from the McQuaid clan. He gave Callie a friendly nod.

With a rather becoming French accent, he said, "Don't worry, I won't tell my German coworkers. I like this little secret competition."

Callie slung the canvas satchel over her shoulder, sighed, and muttered to herself, "So much for a low profile, McQuaid."

CHAPTER 6

The man leaned on the hoe and shielded his eyes against the afternoon sun hanging over the island. His scruffy face was covered in a sheen of sweet. His beer gut strained against his dirty white t-shirt, which was definitely a size too small. He kicked at the soil in the haphazardly growing tomato patch behind his small cottage.

"Well," he said slowly, drawing it out.

Callie could barely contain her annoyance and decided to turn her focus on the landscape around the home. It was beautiful but carried the same eerie energy that she couldn't shake.

The man finally finished his thought. "You wanna go around the property?"

It was then Callie made eye contact with Roy, standing a few feet away. He was alert and intense, scanning the fields around them for Nazis hiding in the tall grass. The two local men he'd brought with him looked just as bored as Callie. They stood around dabbing at their foreheads with handkerchiefs. *These Nova Scotians sure are a sweaty lot,* Callie thought.

"If you're okay with it, we would love to look around," Flint said. "See, we're looking for something, I'm not supposed to call it treasure, but it's treasure. And I remember reading legends about this very spot, your home, and about these strange white rocks that were found- I'm sorry, what's your name, sir?"

"Hall, Jesse Hall. This place was my parent's. I grew up here."

"I'm McQuaid. Flint McQuaid."

"That sounds like a fake name," Jesse Hall said and one of the Nova Scotian roughnecks snorted a laugh into his handkerchief. "I think I know what you're talking about. Big white rock, is that right?"

"It's a very real name, I promise, Jesse. Now it sounds like what you're really trying to get at is, 'What's in it for me?', is that right?"

Jesse didn't answer. He just idly examined a tomato hanging from a vine.

"Well Jesse, first of all I think you'd be entitled to some of that treasure. But even beyond that, you're living in a moment in history right here. That's a very special thing, my friend."

Callie wanted to barf in the dirt between her feet, but Flint actually sounded like he believed it. She couldn't get a hold on the guy. Was he a movie business bozo obsessed with skirt chasing? Did he actually care about what he was doing? If she asked him, she thought, he would probably say both. And he would probably be right. She noticed then that he was wearing white leather wingtip shoes with hand-tooled patterning. Movie business bozo.

Jesse thought about it and said, "I don't give a darn about living history or what not. But treasure, that sounds pretty good."

"Well then, if we find some treasure here, you'll get some. Deal?"

Flint put his hand out. The man wiped sweat off his face and took Flint's hand in his own meaty fist.

"Deal. Let me take you down to the rock and you fellas- and lady- can go from there."

Jesse jammed the blade end of the hoe down into the soft earth and left it standing there. He wandered from his backyard garden out into the tall grass surrounding the property. Flint followed closely behind, then Callie, followed by the local men, and finally Roy, who was still looking out at the horizon with steely eyes, on the lookout for predators.

They walked a couple of hundred yards until Jesse stopped.

“It should be… No, wait. Darn it.”

He grumbled to himself and began walking around them. Callie sidled up next to Flint and together they watched the man shuffle through the grass, kicking and muttering.

“You’ve got the local experts breaking a sweat out here,” she said.

“I have faith in him,” he replied.

A moment of awkward silence followed until Callie asked, “So that was your brother last night?”

They hadn’t spoken after getting back from the bar. Flint had hurried ahead of her on the walk back and then marched into his tent. That morning he’d woken up whistling as if nothing had ever happened.

“Half-brother, technically. Biologically, yes. But as an actual family member, no. He’s nothing to me. I guess that sounds terrible.”

“No, actually… I get it. Family isn’t obligated to stay family, I don’t think.”

“Here it is!” Jesse cried out happily.

The group gathered around to find a large, white rock. It appeared to have been crudely carved into a vaguely tombstone-like shape, though it was unclear if that had been a side effect of rough craftsmanship or everyday weather erosion. Flint stepped closer and planted one of his wingtips into a spot of thick mud.

“God dammit,” Flint growled.

“Hey now, language. We don’t talk about the lord that way,” Jesse chastised him.

"Your rock, your rules," Flint said. Then he said to himself, "Get some normal shoes."

He crouched down in front of the rock and began to examine it. He ran his fingers over its surface and studied where the rock had chipped or worn away, exposing the layers beneath.

"This is a very specific kind of white agate. Native only to Central Europe. It never would have been found here naturally."

"That's a running theme," Callie said.

Flint reached into a small leather pouch attached to his belt and removed a small brush and a scraping tool that Callie had never seen before. Using them both ambidextrously, he was able to clean masses of dried mud from the base of the rock. Something caught his eye. He lay on his stomach in the wet dirt and began to excitedly blow away the remaining fine dust. He gasped, this time for real, and sat up on the balls of his feet.

"It's real. It's real," he said. Then, "Everyone, look."

He stood and backed away, allowing everyone to lean down and take a look at what he had uncovered. Callie went first. There, at the base of the rock, was a cross. It was carved with surprising precision and encircled in an oval. There was something strangely beautiful about it, aside from being simply well crafted. Callie felt a pull, as if it was calling to her.

Without thinking, she looked up at Flint and said, "This is special, isn't it?"

"I think so. What do you think?"

She could only nod, then get out of the way to let the others take a look. Even Major Roy seemed slightly impressed with the finding.

"I had no idea that was there," Jesse said. "All these years… I feel like a real twit. Oh! I just remembered!"

Rather than clarifying anything, Jesse took off, holding his sagging trousers up around his ass as he high stepped it through the tall grass. About a hundred yards away, he stopped. The group watched from a distance as he wandered about in circles again before calling out:

"There's another one! Right here! There's another one!"

"Wait…" Flint said. He looked from the first rock to the second. He said, "Does that second rock look like it's exactly across from the first? What I mean is, does it look like someone is making a line?"

Callie nodded. "What if it's more than a line? What if it's a cross?"

A broad grin broke slowly across Flint's face. "I hate saying this because you've been so damn mean to me, but I think you might be a genius."

"That's going in the script," she said.

"Hey, you fellows of Nova Scotia." Flint pointed at the two locals. "Can you head over there, sorry what's your names?"

"I'm Dylan," said one, a tall, lanky youth. He was barely more than a boy.

"John," said the other, a shorter but no less skinny man. His face was sunburned from work in a field or on a boat.

"Dylan, can you head up that way about… let's double the distance between these… about two hundred yards up that way. Stay in roughly where the center between these two points would be. You're going to be looking for an unusual stone, sort of like these. A totem or monument type of thing. Make sense?"

"You got it, sir!" Dylan nodded and hurried away with the loping gait of an eager golden retriever.

"Okay, John. You head down that way." He gestured in the direction opposite of Dylan. "Let's make it… three hundred yards? Is that right, to make a cross?"

He turned to Callie and Roy. Roy kept his eyes to the tree line surrounding their relatively open field. He didn't look back at Flint but, ever keenly aware, he nodded. Callie looked up from her notebook, where she was jotting down details. The moment felt like something worth documenting.

"That's right, yes," she said.

Flint turned back to John and said, "Okay, so you'll want to-" but John was already on the move, silently trudging away.

"Roy, what do you think about all this?" Flint asked.

Roy held up his hand, silencing him.

"Yes, yes, I couldn't agree more, Major. Thank you for your expertise."

Roy's head turned on his body like a gun turret to face Flint. He was stone-faced, betraying no emotion. Drama was in the air and Callie was excited to see the display. Her pen hovered excitedly over the page…

"My expertise is in keeping you alive, McQuaid. And killing Germans."

"Aren't those kind of the same thing?"

"Flint, in the time that you are taking to distract me with your displays of what I'm sure you believe to be wit, you could be causing me to miss the sun reflecting off of a sniper's scope up in those trees. Or from behind that rock, there. And in the second that I don't catch that flash of light, that sniper could use his German-made Karabiner 98k to send a Mauser 8mm round ripping through your skull with such efficiency that your supposedly ample wit will become nothing more than a fine mist, spraying all over the face of Ms. Carver who is, by the way ma'am, standing much too close to this walking target for safety."

For a long moment Flint and Callie stared at Roy in stunned silence. It was Callie who finally broke it.

"Jesus Christ."

Flint, at a loss for words for the first time in their journey, stammered, "Geez Roy, I uh, I liked you better when you were just eating eggs."

"I am not one of your cocaine-sniffing, cocktail-swilling, do-nothing California gossips. Please do not needlessly distract me from my work."

"Message received," Flint said. Ready to change the subject he called out to Dylan, "Hey pally, you find anything yet?"

Dylan lit up and gave the trio a big wave. "Oh yeah, a couple minutes ago! I didn't know if you wanted me to say!"

Flint sighed. "Where do we find these kids?" he asked under his breath. He called back, "Great job! What is it?"

Dylan cupped his hands around his mouth like a makeshift bullhorn, but it did little to amplify his voice. "It's wide and flat to the ground, not like the others. No markings either… But it's the same kind of rock!"

Flint clapped his hands excitedly. He turned down the field to John and hollered to him.

"John! What do you have?"

"I found that too! Same thing as Dylan! Didn't know if you wanted me to say or not!"

"Is that a Canadian politeness thing?" Callie asked, but Flint was already moving along the line between the two larger rocks.

He stopped exactly in the center of the two lines created by the Nova Scotians. He stared at the ground. His face twisted into a frustrated grimace. He knelt down in the dirt. He removed the small scraper tool and fruitlessly tried to dig into the dirt. Callie watched as, after a minute of getting nowhere, he tossed the tool off to the side and began digging with his hands. She tucked her little notepad into the back pocket of her khaki pants and hurried over to his side. She dropped to her knees and began helping him dig.

"Careful, you're gonna break a nail," he said.

"Shut up."

"What I meant to say was thank you."

"Ow!"

Callie stopped digging and examined her nail. She really had broken one. The middle finger on her right hand. She held it up to show Flint, communicating two things at once.

"I hit something hard down there," she said.

"Yes! Yes!" he said breathlessly and began digging more rapidly.

Despite the pain of her nail, she continued to dig with him. Gradually, they uncovered a large, flat, white stone. Flint pulled the brush from his pouch and Callie watched as he delicately brushed the remaining dirt away from the center of the rock. Little by little, he uncovered an image…

A little lamb. A circular halo behind its head. A flag behind it, emblazoned with a cross.

It was carved with intense detail. Clearly a labor of love by talented hands. Flint traced the image with his dirty index finger and gazed at it in awe.

He whispered, "And looking upon Jesus as he walked, he saith, Behold the Lamb of God."

"I wasn't raised with all this Christian stuff. What does it mean?"

"I wasn't either, it comes with the trade. This is the symbol of John the Baptist."

"John the Baptist as in the magical head that the Knights Templar supposedly prayed to?"

"Yeah… that's the fellow."

Flint believed there was a high chance that the Templar treasure, or the Head of John the Baptist, or whatever the island may contain, was hidden below the stone. It was a much more subtle marker than the Money Pit, which was feeling more and more like an intentional distraction.

He wanted to start digging right that instant. He wiped the sweat off his brow and squinted at the late afternoon sun. It was slowly lowering into evening. The rest of the crew looked worn out. He wondered how long it would take to get everyone mobilized and set up with the necessary digging tools. They couldn't work in the dark.

The next day, bright and early, they'd be out digging.

***

That night, Flint couldn't sleep. He tossed and turned on his cot. He soaked his t-shirt and boxers with sweat. His thoughts raced and his limbs felt like an electrical current was coursing through them. He groaned and punched his pillow into shape. He wished he was back in his bed, back in the comfort he'd come to love. As exhilarating as being back on the hunt had been, it was moments like these that reminded him why he had traded in adventuring for Egyptian cotton sheets.

Then he heard it: A voice, whispering his name. It sounded vaguely feminine, though he couldn't be sure. *Callie*? he wondered. For a moment the idea that she was calling to him in the night excited him. He pushed the feeling out of his mind. He had no idea what she actually thought of him. For that matter, he didn't know how he felt about her. It was complicated, and he didn't like complicated.

It came again. "*Flint? Flint?*" The voice sounded desperate. The whispers were haunting.

He rose from the cot and felt a strange heaviness in his body. An exhaustion permeated him, a tiredness so depleting that it felt somehow permanent. It was difficult to walk to his shoes, like his bare feet were somehow covered in lead. Flint pushed through the feeling and forced himself to move. He slipped his feet into the ruined white wingtips. He winced as he discovered they were full to the brim with mud. *How had that happened?*

He moved stiffly through the flap door of his tent and took in the campsite around him. It was totally dead. No fire. No watchman. Some of the tent flaps were open, revealing that the tents were actually empty, not even full of silently sleeping crew members. The air was strangely humid. Balmy and cloying. He felt like he was back in the jungles of Guatemala, not the woods of Nova Scotia.

"*Flint? Flint?*" The voice came again, this time from somewhere in the forest surrounding their campsite.

Flint followed the voice into the trees. He didn't think about it, he just did. It was as if the voice were carrying him along, magically. He thought of Callie's assessment of the island. The creepy pull it had over her. Was this his own mystical awakening to the island's power?

He peered through the leaves and branches, trying to make out where the voice was coming from. Three small, green lights floated in formation amongst the trees. The lights were a bright green. Flint actually found them to be pleasant. Just as inviting as the voice.

He followed the lights, transfixed. They carried him deeper into the woods and he stumbled over rocks and fallen trees, but he kept moving after them. When they began to move faster, he quickened his pace. When they raced away from him, he sprinted, leaping over obstructions with an agility that surprised him.

Then, the lights disappeared.

Flint stopped. He looked around at his surroundings for the first time since setting eyes on the otherworldly lights. He was in a small clearing. A heavy mist hung around the edges, nearly obscuring the trees around him. He wasn't sure where he was, but somehow he knew that it was very far away from the campsite. Far away from help.

Slowly, two figures emerged from the opposite sides of the clearing. At first, as they moved through the shadows, their faces appeared to Flint as his own. It wasn't until they stepped fully into the moonlight that Flint realized that they were his father and brother.

He tried to speak. To scream at them. But nothing came out. His voice was trapped in his chest.

Nolan smiled at him. Declan did not.

"Come here, my son. Come to us," Nolan said softly.

His voice carried a kindness, a warmth, that Flint hadn't remembered from his boyhood. His father opened his arms in an invitation to embrace.

Slowly, cautiously, Flint approached the two men. His legs felt heavier than ever. He felt the mud in his wingtips suction at his feet. But still, he pushed on. He wanted, more than anything, to hug his father.

It wasn't until he reached the very center of the clearing that the ground gave way beneath him. The earth seemed to open up and swallow him and he fell through the air into a pitch-black maw, landing painfully on a dirt floor. Wincing and gasping for breath, he stood up and tried to get his bearings.

He was in a deep, cylindrical pit, surrounded on all sides by hard, dirt walls. Sticks and leaves at his feet told him that he'd stepped onto a boobytrap, a covering to camouflage the opening of the pit. It had given away instantly under his weight.

He looked up and there they were, his father and brother. They stood next to each other, peering down at him. Now Declan was smiling, too.

"Please," Flint pleaded. "Please help me out of here."

He hated asking for their help, but he felt he had no other choice. Nolan, still grinning at him, now almost manically, shook his head.

"Oh, son. Don't you understand yet? You're never going anywhere."

CHAPTER 7

"You're not going anywhere. You're not going anywhere," Nolan said.

Then Declan began the chant as well. "You're not going anywhere. You're not going anywhere."

The two men's voices spoke in unison, again and again, creating a repetitive mantra that echoed down into the pit, magnifying around Flint, growing louder and louder with each word.

Flint covered his ears and closed his eyes. He screamed to drown them out. He screamed as long and loud as he could.

Then he began to hear another voice bleed through over the cacophony.

"Flint? Flint? Flint?"

It was the soft, feminine voice from before. This time, it sounded like it was definitely Callie.

"Flint? Flint? Flint?"

The sound of his name being called rose above all the other voices until it was all that he could hear.

Flint opened his eyes.

He was right back where he started. Lying on his cot and covered in flop sweat. Callie was kneeling by his bed. She was gripping his arm tightly, shaking him awake. He sat upright and looked around, stricken with panic and fear.

"Where am I? What- What are you doing?!" he screamed.

She rose and stepped away from his bed, her hands raised in the air to show she was no threat. She spoke to him in a calming whisper.

"I came to get you and you were going cuckoo in here. Screaming in your sleep. You were having a nightmare or something but you're okay now."

He flopped back on the cot and tried to catch his breath. He was still hyperventilating a bit. Callie approached his bedside, again with her hands up and open.

"What were you dreaming about?"

He didn't answer. How could he explain what had happened between them all on that day? How could he show himself as the boy that his own father didn't want? He knew that once he revealed that to anyone, they wouldn't want him either. Not as a lover, as a friend, not even as a so-called expert in his field.

When Callie realized she wasn't going to get a response, she said, "Well, you're safe now, old boy."

"What did you come to talk to me about?"

"Huh?" Callie had completely forgotten why she'd actually come to wake him up.

"Why are you here?" Irritation was creeping into his voice. He was embarrassed and wanted her out as soon as possible.

"Oh yeah! Right. I came here to ask you, no, tell you, that we're going to explore the Money Pit. Together. Right now."

"What, are you off your nut? I'm exhausted, I can't think straight. I'm not traipsing around in the night."

She moved to the edge of the cot and sat down.

"With your crumb of a Nazi brother out there digging around, this is the only time we stand a chance of exploring it. You and I both know you wanna get in there."

Flint groaned. "I already told you. I think the Money Pit is just a sideshow. I mean, how over the top can you get?"

"You said it yourself, it's the source of the whole mystery! Whatever the reality of it might be, it's the starting point. And we should at least know everything the Nazis know, shouldn't we?"

She was right. He wanted to crawl under the bed and hide. He wanted to be back home in his pool where he didn't have to deal with Declan or Nazis or any of the rest of it. Still, Callie's excited smile was making a case.

"Yes, I admit it, you've even got me excited about this little mystery. Besides, it's moments like these that will make our big screen debut exciting. I'm already working on the scene in my head. It's gonna be a good one. Oh, and I forgot!"

With her long legs it took just two strides to get to the other side of the tent. She reached through the flap and pulled in a pair of worn leather work boots.

"I estimated your size. I swiped them from out front of some other fellow's tent, so they're hot."

Flint laughed but shook his head. "I appreciate the passion, but you're dingy! I mean totally whacky if you think I'm going out there right now. If I don't get enough sleep my face gets all puffy in the morning."

"That's bull, McQuaid. You really think you're going back to sleep?"

She tossed the boots at him, squared her shoulders, and crossed her arms.

"You and I both know you're going out there with me."

***

Flint and Callie were about half a mile away from the campsite when they realized they were being followed. The duo exchanged silent glances in the moonlight, but kept walking. Every few steps they would hear the faintest of sounds. A rustle. A twig snapping. The sounds were barely detectable, but they were on such high alert that they caught them. Flint mouthed the words, "*Keep going,*" then darted into the trees.

He hid behind the wide trunk of an ancient red oak. He watched as Callie continued walking alone. He held his breath. Just before she vanished into the forest, he saw a large, dark figure emerge from behind some foliage. Flint couldn't make out the face, but it was undoubtedly a man. A rifle was slung over his shoulder and the knife in his hand glinted in the white light of the moon. The figure followed after Callie from a distance. Flint estimated him to be about fifteen yards behind. Given the darkness of the forest, it was far enough away that the guy couldn't actually see Callie, just as she couldn't see him. He was tracking by sound.

Flint crept out and fell in-line behind them. He carefully stepped at the exact time that the other man did, so that their footfalls fell in unison. Strategically, he took longer strides so that he covered more ground and gained on the man. It didn't take long before the creeper was within arm's reach…

Flint lunged forward and threw his left arm around the man's neck. The man gasped in the dark and immediately tensed up. Flint could tell the guy was powerfully built. He was in for a fight. He then clapped his right hand over the guy's mouth to muffle his cries for help. The man was fighting wildly, trying to shake Flint off of him. He was doing a damn good job of it.

"Callie, help!" Flint hissed in the dark.

Callie wheeled around and was immediately on the shadowy figure, punching him repeatedly in the stomach with the skill of a boxer. Flint was quietly impressed. But the man wasn't going down without a fight. He slapped Callie across the face and, when that didn't work, grabbed both of her arms to try and subdue her. She was strong and aggressive enough to rip from his grasp, but not before he tore one of her shirt sleeves at the shoulder.

It wasn't until the creep bit Flint's hand that Flint uncovered his mouth, allowing the man to bellow out, "It's me, you idiots!"

The voice had a familiar ring.

"Major Roy?" Callie asked.

"Yes, you dingy dame! Who did you think it was?"

"Um, how about a Nazi assassin? What were we supposed to think? It's pitch black out here," Flint, carefully to not alert any real Nazi assassins.

"I saw you leaving the camp and I wanted to come and help protect you. Good thing I did, too, given your collective attack skills."

"Call me a dingy dame again and you're gonna get another rabbit punch, Nazi or no," Callie said tersely.

Flint then noticed her torn sleeve. Roy was already staring. It had ripped exactly at the shoulder and had fallen, settling in a limp bunch at her wrist. Her entire arm was exposed. It was covered, from her wrist to her shoulders, in colorful tattoos. Flowers and birds, a lucky horseshoe, and a heart with an arrow through it. She tried to pull the sleeve up, but it fell uselessly back down again.

"What are you looking at?" she grumbled at them. "Nothing," Roy said.

"Nothing at all," Flint replied.

"Let's just keep moving," Callie said.

***

Thirty minutes later, Callie and Flint were standing at the edge of the Money Pit, staring down into the inky black void. Major Roy was positioned in a tree a couple of hundred yards away, keeping watch. Flint turned and waved at the tree.

"What are you doing?" Callie asked.

“Saying hi to Roy,” he said cheerfully.

They spoke in hushed tones so as not to let their voices carry across the open field where the Money Pit lay.

“We need to stay focused, McQuaid.”

“We also need to thank our friends when they do a good job. Like, for instance, when they stop someone from sneaking up and murdering you.”

“Oh, you mean Roy?”

“You were with me, you dingy dame.”

She glared at him for a moment before saying, “Fine. Thank you.”

“You’re welcome.”

Flint knelt down at the edge of the hole. He peered down into the darkness, trying to make out anything at all. He fingered a pebble out of the dirt and tossed it down. They listened to its journey. After a much longer fall than Flint liked, the little rock let out a light *ping* and then settled.

“That sounded deeper than I would like,” Flint said.

“If that was a suggestion that I should go down instead, I’m going to ignore it.”

“No, I need you on belay. One of us has to monitor in case of emergency and I trust you more than myself.”

Flint dug around the canvas satchel that they had brought along and removed a one-hundred-yard length of rope, a mallet, and several steel climbing pitons. He took ten paces back from the edge of the pole and, using the mallet, drove the first piton into the ground. He fed the end of the rope through the piton’s anchor hole and tied it off in a bowline knot. He then moved back toward the hole, stopping to do the same thing every three feet. When done, he stepped back and examined his work. Three safety catches dug into the ground. He jerked on the rope, and they held firm.

He tried to wrap and tie the other end of the rope around his torso under his armpits so he could lower himself down. He struggled to get the line around himself and kept dropping it.

Callie stepped in to help, wrapping the rope, and her arms, around him. Having her arms around him gave Flint a warm feeling in his gut. He tried to ignore it. Instead, he focused on tying the rope together while she held it in place. When the knot was ready, she stepped away.

"Looks good," she said. "And if it fails, I'll be here to hold tight."

"I believe you," he said, and he did. He looked down into the Money Pit again. "This is a bit of a confined space, isn't it? Not all that spacious."

"You're not scared, are you?"

"No, this is no big thing. Hell, I'm excited. This'll be juicy!" He took a deep breath and shook his limbs. He was not excited. Something occurred to him, then. He said, "We got here pretty easily, didn't we? To the Money Pit, I mean? No guards or anything… A little strange, don't you think?"

"Stop making excuses," she said.

She knew he was right; it was a bit strange that the Germans didn't have at least one of their soldiers protecting their research work. Still, she didn't want to dwell on it, if for no other reason than it was delaying their progress and making them more vulnerable.

"You're right, fine."

Callie pulled a pair of brown leather gloves from her back pocket and pulled them on. She took up the other end of the rope with both hands, ready to help feed him enough slack as he rappelled downward.

Flint winked at Callie and gave her a salute.

"Abyssinia, kid," he said.

"Abyssinia, McQuaid. Good luck."

With that, he stepped over the edge and rappelled down into the darkness. As she watched him disappear into the pit, worry gnawed at her. She had a bad feeling, and it was getting worse.

Down in the Money Pit, Flint moved with as much delicacy and precision as he could muster, planting one foot after the other against the soft wet earth that made up the hole's walls. Roots broke free from the walls and insects crawled along the surface. Roaches, beetles, centipedes, they all hissed and squirmed and jockeyed over one another. Flint shuddered in revulsion.

"Here's to hoping the Knights Templar built a nice little speakeasy down here…" he muttered to himself.

His boot hit a slick rock in the soil and slipped out from under him. He nearly lost his footing but managed to right himself at the last moment. He was grateful to Callie for picking up the slack. And for being the only reason he wasn't tumbling through the air.

His boots touched down on firm ground. He shook off the rope harness and gave it a tug to let Callie know he had landed. She tugged back. Knowing she was up there made him feel safer, more confident, even as he looked around and realized the pit was a much tighter fit than he'd thought. Roughly eight feet by eight feet. It wasn't a coffin, but it didn't make him feel any safer.

He took a deep breath and shook it off.

He rooted about in his satchel until he found what he needed: his flashlight. A simple black metal cylinder with "Eveready" stamped on the side. He pressed the button forward and the light came to life in his hand. He thought about the days when archaeologists had to navigate places like this one with actual flaming torches and shook his head. He was lucky to be alive during a more advanced time with flashlights and moving pictures and personal massage tools. *God I miss Los Angeles right now*, he thought.

He was thinking about what that batty mask girl was up to when something caught his eye. Fabric scraps on the ground. He knelt down and got a closer look. The floor itself was made from a layer of expertly laid oak logs. They were packed so tightly and filled in with muddy dirt that he could shine his flashlight between the logs to see what was beneath. Whoever created this multi-layered pit knew what they were doing.

Next, he turned his attention to the fabric itself. It was a thick, fibrous, organic material. Coconut fiber. All the way in Nova Scotia.

"How in the hell did you get all the way here?" he whispered. Then, "Why am I talking to a bit of coconut?"

He pocketed a bit of the coconut fiber. He hoped the Nova Scotian soil embedded in it might help act as some kind of proof when they returned from their journey. *If* they returned, he corrected himself.

He moved his flashlight slowly along the surface of the pit. At first he found nothing but more dirt and bugs. Then, something caught his eye. Something glittering in a pile of rocks and soil and wooden beams along the wall opposite him. Something golden.

"Looks like the Money Pit is going to provide…" he said.

Flint hurried to the pile and took a closer look. It was around six feet high and roughly three feet in width. The more he studied the wooden beams and rocks, the more they appeared to have been structural. They looked like they had once lined a doorway and held up the earth to create a ceiling. There had been a doorway there, a tunnel leading somewhere underground, but it had collapsed. Judging by the rot of the wooden beams, Flint believed it had fallen down many years ago. He shuddered at the thought of some poor soul being trapped in the debris.

Dropping to his knees before the pile, he began to sift carefully through the detritus. He focused on unearthing the sliver of gold that he had uncovered first. As he shifted the rocks and decaying wood out of the way he discovered that what he had hoped was a golden coin was more. Much more.

He soon revealed that what had been glittering in the dark was actually the pommel of a massive broadsword. Flint pulled the sword out. It was so heavy, he had to hold it with both hands to examine it properly. He tucked the flashlight awkwardly between his chin and collarbone so that he could hold it hands-free and get a closer look.

Engraved in the rusting blade were the Latin words: "*Non Nobis, Domine, Non Nobis, Sed Nomini Tuo Ad Gloriam.*" Translated to English, Flint knew it meant "*Nothing for us, Lord, nothing for us but for the glory of thy name.*" The creed of the Knights Templar.

Carefully, Flint laid it next to him on the oak floor. He continued to dig until he thought he heard something groan. It was faint, but it sounded human. Flooded with panic, Flint dug furiously. Was it possible that the collapse was more recent than he thought? Could someone be alive down there?

He dug until he uncovered a man lying in the rubble. The man's skin was deathly pale, the whitest Flint had ever seen. He was clad in fabric and leather and chain mail that was distinctly medieval. All of his clothing had rotted and rusted. It appeared to Flint to be centuries-old. The man's face was drawn and sunken. His eyes were open wide, staring up at nothing. His mouth hung open to reveal rotting nubs of teeth and a swollen purple tongue. The odor coming off of him was shocking.

He seemed so obviously dead, and yet he wasn't decayed… Could he have moaned?

Flint waved his hand in front of the man's eyes. He didn't blink. He held his hand in front of the man's mouth. No breathing. The last thing he wanted to do was actually touch the man, but it was the only way to absolutely confirm death. Tentatively, Flint reached out and took the man's thin wrist in between his index and middle fingers and his thumb. He pressed his fingers lightly against the man's radial artery, feeling for a pulse.

Nothing.

Flint dropped the man's arm and it fell limply to the ground.

He couldn't make any sense of it. He had heard that these kinds of preservations were possible in extreme conditions, peat bogs and Arctic cold and the like. But he knew there was no way that a body would have survived intact in a moist, insect-filled environment like the Money Pit.

Then the man blinked.

Flint fell backwards and scrambled away until he hit the wall behind him. He would have screamed but it caught in his throat. He couldn't yell, he couldn't even breathe.

The man's slack mouth came together around his engorged tongue, and he croaked out a sentence in French.

"En quelle… année… sommes-nous?"

Flint's French was rusty to non-existent, and he wasn't going to wait around to ask for clarification. He bolted to the wall where his rope was hanging and yanked as hard as he could.

"Callie! Callie, pull me up! Pull me up!" he screamed. "Now, dammit!"

No tugs came back. No pull to help him back up the wall. *Oh no.*

The man groaned incoherently and reached out toward him with a hand so thin it was nearly skeletal. The fingernails had sloughed off long ago and left bloody, scabbed tips at the end. Despite his broken state, the man began to pull the debris away. He was working to free himself.

"Not only am I trapped in a box again, I'm in a box with the monster from *White Zombie*," he said to himself in a terrified whisper.

Desperate, Flint slipped the rope around himself. He pulled on the rope until all of the slack fell down and coiled at his feet. Now the rope was at least completely taut, and he could use it to leverage his climb upward. He planted his feet on the wall and, with every ounce of his strength, began to pull his way up the wall.

He never thought that he would look back at the incident with Declan and Nolan in Egypt with rose tinted glasses, but at least then he had crampons.

The man in the Money Pit began shrieking at him in a mixture of French and guttural nonsense.

Flint kept his eyes closed until he reached the mouth of the pit. As soon as he stepped onto flat earth he pulled the rope off and fell to his knees.

"Callie, where the hell were you?!"

"Right here, Flint."

When he looked up to find her, he came face to face with the barrel of a German rifle.

Callie and Roy were standing in front of him, surrounded by several Nazi soldiers, including the creep that had bumped into them in the bar, Sauer.

“Oh, hey fellas. How are we this evening?” Flint asked. He turned to Callie. “Nice warning.”

“They had a lot of guns pointed at me, Flint.”

Sauer barked an order at Obersoldat Baldur Axmann, who was standing at nervous attention nearby. The young soldier hurried to Flint. He grabbed him by the arm and forced him to his feet.

Flint gave Roy the evil eye and said, “Looks like you boys were able to breach our security perimeter, huh?”

“This is not the first time the Huns have captured me,” Roy said to Flint. Then, he addressed his German captors. “I wonder if it was your fathers whose graves I dug on that day. What a joy it will be to chop down another branch of their family tree.”

The soldiers, most of whom seemed to know a bit of English, all looked at each other uncomfortably.

“He’s a little intense. You’ll get used to that,” Flint said. “In the meantime, there’s something down in that pit. Something that looks like Bela Lugosi brought it back to life.”

“What?” Callie asked, incredulously.

Sauer growled another order at Baldur. The kid went to the edge of the pit. He looked into the darkness, listening intently. Nothing. He turned back to Sauer and shrugged.

“Shut up,” Sauer said in a thick German accent. “Now you come with me. Now you give us answers, Yankee swine.”

CHAPTER 8

The farmhouse was quaint. Cute, even. It seemed to be a rather inappropriate place to be tortured and killed, which was what Flint assumed the Nazis had in store for them. He, Callie and Roy had all be roughly tied and unceremoniously sat down in three rickety old chairs with sagging wooden bottoms. The man that stood before them in the long, black leather coat and the rictus grin looked familiar. It took Flint a moment to place him.

"Oh, you're the fellow from the bar! The creepy one with the terrible face. That's where I know you from. How've you been, pally?"

Sauer didn't say anything. He let his beady eyes rove over his three captives while muttering in German under his breath. Flint noticed that the kid standing guard nearby seemed extremely uneasy around his SS boss. He kept glancing from the guy to a framed painting of Jesus Christ that hung on the wall. The only piece of artwork that Flint could see in the living room where they were being housed. He wondered whose farmhouse they had set themselves up in. He wondered if the poor soul was still alive. Then Sauer pointed at Roy.

He said, "You there. You are the most interesting to me. Let us go to the bedroom where we may… chat."

A hand emerged from his coat pocket holding a switchblade. *Snikt*. The blade popped to life in his hand and gleamed even in the low light of the room's oil lamp. He approached Roy and grabbed him by the shirt, forcing him to his feet. The SS officer was stronger than he looked. Roy struggled, but with his hands tied behind his back, there was little he could do. Especially after Sauer pressed the tip of the blade against his ribs.

"Get off of me, you goddamn Kraut!" Roy hollered.

Sauer wasn't listening. He dragged Roy away into an adjoining bedroom and kicked the door shut.

Callie murmured low under breath. "Flint, you don't happen to speak German, do you?"

"I actually do a little bit. My crumb of an old man moved there and made a little German family. I tried to learn it. Then realized I was wasting my time." He turned to the young soldier. "Hey there, kid. Er, kinder!"

The kid looked at him with wide, worried eyes. He was gripping his rifle very tightly with shaking hands. Flint hoped he wasn't as trigger happy as he seemed.

"Darf ich muttermilch trinken?" Flint produced each word with great intention but still sounded like he was chewing each syllable.

The soldier replied in perfect English, "You just asked me if you could be freed to drink breast milk."

"Oh, you speak a little German, huh Flint?" Callie grumbled.

"I don't know, I was trying to say motherland. You speak English, kid?"

The kid nodded.

"What's your name?"

He cleared his throat, trying to sound confident, adult. "Obersoldat Baldur Axmann."

"You like the movies, Obersoldat Baldur Axmann?"

The kid nodded again.

"You cut these ropes around our wrists and help us get our monster bodyguard free and we'll get you a starring role with Loretta Young. You like Loretta Young? I have her phone number."

"Trust me, sir. Whatever Loretta Young might do to me would not be worth it compared to what Sauer will do to me."

Flint snorted a laugh. Even Callie broke out a small grin. The humorous moment dissipated when they heard Roy bellow from in the adjoining room. It wasn't a scream, but a loud, deep, painful bark. Like a wounded dog who was fighting to stay brave but couldn't hold it back any longer. Whatever Sauer was doing to him, Flint knew he wanted no part in it.

"That's funny. I like you, kiddo. Do you know my brother? He's an archaeologist like me. He's traveling with you all."

"Declan?" Baldur asked.

"That's the one. The one and only. He's a bit of a prick."

The kid shifted uncomfortably. He looked around nervously, unsure of what to say.

"He seems like a nice gentleman to me," he said eventually.

"He's not. He's a prick. But he's not a psychopath like that guy in there is. You know he's a psychopath, right? Seems like the real violent kind too once he gets his meat hooks on you. Judging by our friend's noises, at least. You don't seem like a psycho either, Baldur. In fact, you seem like kind of an alright guy for a Nazi. I mean, you stuck up for my twit of a brother."

The kid was listening now. He was focused, no longer nervously moving about. His rifle was lowered to his side. Flint could tell he wanted to do the right thing. He knew he had almost won him over.

"I know you can't untie us. I know you can't let us get away or even go in there blasting like Jimmy Cagney. But you can go get my brother. Bring him in here and let's pray to God that he can talk some sense into this maniac. Will you do that for us?"

Flint searched Baldur's face, finding the sympathy there, the compassion. He knew the young man was about to break when Roy let out another piercing howl. Then Baldur turned and ran out of the farmhouse.

***

Declan tapped the end of his pen against his teeth and felt the tiny vibrations rattle up into his skull. There was something comforting about it to him. Something he didn't understand and couldn't explain. Just another of his "strange ticks," as his father would call them. He had always been after Declan for his eccentric behaviors. Declan knew that his father was right, of course. People didn't like those that were too different. Odd or flamboyant behavior drew the wrong kind of attention. Told people that you weren't a serious man.

Just look at Flint, he thought as he leaned back in the captain's chair the soldiers had set up in his enormous standing tent. Talk about flamboyant behavior. Those ridiculous clothes and little mustache and Hollywoodland attitude. It all explained why he was no longer a serious member of the archeological community. At least he hadn't been…

He couldn't fathom how his half-brother had gotten involved in the expedition, but it frustrated him. This was supposed to be his dig, his moment to shine, and then here was Flint coming back into his life to make things more complicated and take his spotlight. Still, there was a small part of him that was glad his brother had come. He now had an opportunity to prove once and for all to his father that he was the superior son. To assure him that he had made the right choice that day in the pyramid.

Declan knew he had received a tremendous honor and been gifted a great opportunity by being allowed to lead the archeological side of the expedition, but he thought it a shame that the expedition was funded by the Nazi party. He didn't care for the party's rise in his homeland. All the heiling and Führer nonsense. Their ideas about purity and eugenics made him uncomfortable, but as far as he knew it was all talk.

Still, he knew that no other government in the world was funding the kind of research into historical occult and religious artifacts as Hitler was. It was impossible to say no to the kind of expedition he had been handed. Not that he could have if he'd wanted to. His father would have made him go no matter what. It was just too great an opportunity, even if it was assigned to him by a flamboyant, un-serious man like Hitler.

He realized that his mind had been wandering and he was still tapping the pen against his incisors. He was supposed to be writing a letter to his father, updating him on the progress of the dig. Declan considered mentioning Flint's appearance but decided against it. No, he would handle his half-brother on his own.

Just as he set his pen to paper, Baldur burst into his tent. The young soldier was wide-eyed and breathless.

"Declan, please, you need to come with me," he said between labored puffs. "They've captured your brother."

***

Flint and Callie sat in tense silence and listened to the sounds emanating from the other room. Shortly after Baldur left, the whirring sound of some kind of machine had started up. Roy had let out a series of grunts and groans but was stronger than Sauer had ever anticipated. They could tell as the German's voice had become louder and more demanding. It sounded as if he was becoming furious with his inability to break Roy.

The duo knew they didn't have to say it out loud. They were both thinking the same thing: *"I hope he doesn't get bored with Roy and come for one of us before help arrives."*

Flint broke the uncomfortable silence, saying, "So… your tattoos. What's the story behind those?"

Callie stopped struggling against her ropes for a moment.

"Is this a good time to talk about our personal histories?"

"Just trying to make conversation. This is a little bit awkward, after all."

"Awkward? It sounds like he's killing poor Roy in there!" Callie said against clenched teeth as she tried to work her way out of her bindings.

"I realize that," Flint said. "Again, just trying to keep things light. Besides, this could be your last chance to reveal yourself to another human being."

"Seeing my shoulder is about as revealing as I'm going to get with you."

She gave up on the knot around her wrist. She slumped back in the chair, exhausted and worried. She winced as she heard Roy let out a yelp.

"Fine. I'll tell you. I grew up in Nebraska. On a farm. Just another small-town girl."

"All-American! You oughta be in pictures, you know?"

"Oh, hush. I worked the farm with my family. Me and my mom, my dad, and my brother, Henry. Then one day, Henry got sick. Dysentery from drinking out of a river nearby. He… it happened so quickly. He was just gone. My dad went right after that. Just a few months later.

"They said it was a heart attack, but I know the truth. He'd lost his son. He loved me, but I couldn't be what he wanted. The way he loved Henry, it was different. Stronger. Almost mystical or something. I know his heart was just broken. He couldn't go on.

"My mother is tough. Smart. She handled all of the business for the farm, and I'm good with my hands. I can bale hay. I can hoe and plant. But there were only two of us, we couldn't keep the farm going that way. We needed help. We invited my uncle, my mom's brother, to come stay with us. He was a ranch hand, never had a real place of his own, so he came.

"My father was a good man. He was kind and respectful. He was a gentleman. My uncle… wasn't.

"One day, a circus came through town. I snuck away and went. I think I was around twelve years old. Maybe thirteen. I loved the animals and the comedians. Most of all, I loved the acrobats. They risked everything to show the world who they were and what they could do. And all of them, no matter what they did, were totally free. I got to talking to the barker and he said they could always use extra hands, so when they left, I went with them.

"I set up tents and shoveled elephant shit. But eventually, if you want to stay, you have to prove you're one of them. You had to really do something to contribute. I'd always admired the tattoos on some of the men, so I got one. Then another and another. Eventually I covered every part of me. Almost every part, anyway. From my ankles to my wrists. I became the tattooed lady.

"The whole time I was writing stories. Most of them about my travels around the country, the people I'd met. A lot of adventures with elephants or crime stories set in the small towns of America. I sold a lot to the pulps under the fake names of men. Brick Danworth was my most popular pseudonym.

"One day I got a letter from Weissbaum. He'd been reading my stories and he wanted to hire me. To this day I have no idea how he found out my real name or how he got the address to contact me. We were in a new town every few days. But he took a chance with the tattooed lady."

Flint was stunned. He thought he had had a wild ride of a life, but hers was even more eventful. He'd never met anyone who'd lived as much as she had.

"Well, that explains the outfits," he said.

"Shut up," she said.

"I'm joking, I'm sorry. That's incredible. If you'd asked me to guess I would have never gotten there in a million years. I think I understand why you fight the way you do, now."

"Thank you. I appreciate it."

The creaking of the farmhouse's front door announced the arrival of Baldur and Declan. The first thing that Flint noticed when they entered the living room was Declan's wide, smug grin. He strode to the middle of the room and stood there with his legs spread a bit, his arms crossed, smirking at Flint and Callie. The forced power stance made Callie cringe. It enraged Flint.

"You might be the acknowledged son, but you're still a bastard," Flint said.

"Oh, come now," Declan said in his light German accent. "That's no way to talk to your brother."

"Half-brother. Don't forget that."

"Well, I'm the closest thing to family that you have in this room. In your whole life, from what I hear from Father. He still keeps tabs on you for some reason. I suppose he's a masochist. Do you know what he calls you, Flint? The saddest man in Hollywoodland. Has a nice ring to it." Declan turned to Callie. "You there, miss. How much did he pay you to be his friend?"

That remark shut Flint down. He hung his head. Callie suddenly saw just how vulnerable Flint really was. Beneath all the Los Angeles, lothario bravado, he was a wounded, lonely man.

"Leave him alone and let us go." Callie spat at Declan's feet.

"I'm afraid I can't just do that." He pulled a handkerchief form his back pocket and casually wiped the spit from his boot.

"Declan, please." Flint's voice was hoarse. He sounded ground down. Broken, even. He spoke with more conviction than she'd thought capable. "I know you hate me. Lord knows I loathe you. But right now, there's a man in that room being tormented by your rabid coworker. He's being tortured for information about our hunt that he probably doesn't even have. And if he does, he's certainly never going to part with it. It's pointless brutality and you can stop it."

Something in the words seemed to hit Declan. He knew his brother was right, but to admit that would be to relinquish the control he had.

"Well, that would technically be an SS matter. I'm not his superior. It's a bureaucracy issue," Declan said.

"I want to believe that you're not really like the rats. Please. Prove me right."

Flint didn't actually know if Declan had given himself over to Hitler's crew of thugs or not. But no matter what Declan felt in his dark heart, Flint knew that if nothing else, admitting defeat to Declan would be satisfying enough to win him over.

He said, "You got me, okay? Tell Dad whatever you want. Laugh about me together. You win. Just please stop this and let us go."

For a moment, Declan listened to the ominous sounds emanating from behind the door. He chewed his lip in a show of faux consideration.

“Hm… alright. We don’t need to turn this into an international incident. Sauer is a cultural moron who doesn’t understand that everyone goes batty when something happens to you movie industry types. …One condition, though.”

“What do you want?” Flint snapped.

Declan stepped toward Flint with a mechanical intentionality. He didn’t stop until he was standing over him. He looked down at him with that same irritating grin. Flint could feel his hot breath on his face. He locked eyes with his brother.

“As soon as we let you go, you return to your camp and pack up. By the time the sun has risen tomorrow, you are vanished, like a ghost. You never return to our profession and sully it with your name. You all give up, and never look back.”

Without breaking eye contact with Declan, Flint growled, “Fine.”

Declan stepped back and chuckled. “Well, that was easy! You have a deal, Brother!” He clapped Baldur on the back in a chummy way. “Go help these two with their ropes. I’ll go and see if I can talk this attack dog into putting the muzzle back on.”

CHAPTER 9

Callie stood in the middle of the swirling chaos of their campsite as the Nova Scotians tore it down. All around her, tents and traveling furniture were being disassembled. Weapons and tools were packed away. Trucks had been brought in as close as possible to the heavily wooded campsite. They were waiting to get loaded up and drive them back to the mainland where a private plane had been chartered to bring them back to the US.

The sun had barely begun to rise over the trees of Oak Island, but already the day was over. The movie deal, the quest for treasure and knowledge, the search was over. She felt powerless, dragged out to sea by the tide.

"Hey! What's going on?" a small but forceful voice cut through the noise.

Callie looked to find Shirley at the edge of camp, waving her hands in the air. She ran toward Callie, dodging moving men wielding luggage and tentpoles. When she arrived she looked up and fixed Callie with those big, hungry eyes.

"What's happening?" she asked.

Callie knelt down so that she could look Shirley in the eye. She brushed the windswept hair out of the girl's face.

"We have to leave," she said.

"But… but I wanted to help," Shirley said.

"I know. I did too."

Those hungry eyes began to well with tears.

"Oh, come here, sweetie. It's okay."

Callie pulled her close and wrapped her arms around her. She wanted to cry herself, but couldn't. She didn't want the men around her to see her break down. She also knew, from years of experience, that crying didn't solve anything. Still, she couldn't help but feel destroyed over the knowledge that the abusers, the bullies, the bad guys, call them whatever you want, were going to win. That was when she reminded herself that she was not powerless.

She pulled away from Shirley and slipped a ten-dollar bill into her coat pocket. She told her that it wasn't over and to always be brave, no matter what. Then she sent the girl home.

When she walked into Flint's tent, he was packing up with feverish speed. Throwing his high-end clothing into designer leather bags, grabbing books and stacking them in a steamer trunk. He seemed almost unhinged.

"Flint," Callie said. He didn't respond. Louder, she called out, "Flint!"

He stopped, his arms full of digging tools. He looked at her like she was an alien, some strange force that wasn't supposed to be standing in front of him in that moment.

"What?" he asked, tersely.

"We can't go. We have to finish this," she implored.

He shook his head and went back to packing. He tried to get the tools situated in a special side bag, but he was frustrated and moving too quickly, and he couldn't get them to fit where they belonged.

He said, "You know Roy is in the medical tent. That maniac really did a number on him. He burned him with a snipe! More too, I'm sure. Poor guy."

"We can't let them win like this, Flint. You know it too. This isn't right. We have to fight here. I mean, let's say this thing, the Head of John the Baptist, let's say it's actually real. What if it really did fall into the hands of the Nazis? If they did that to Roy, what do you think they'll do to the world with that kind of power?"

Flint's frustrated packing came to a head and, in a moment of rage, he flung a small digging spade across the tent, where it clattered to the floor. He turned to Callie, his face a pinched mess of emotion. Anger, sadness, regret.

"Don't you get it? Declan is right! My father is right! I'm a loser. I can't do this. I haven't even been out in the field in years. This whole thing has been a disaster, I don't know what I'm doing. I'm just a movie fraud. Even my relationships are fake, for God's sake! And now we're up against Nazis and a… a… a zombie man down in a tunnel and…" He stopped like a train that ran out of coal and just can't keep chugging. "You knew it when you first met me on set, Callie. I'm just a loser. A phony. Admit it."

Callie took his hands in hers. She spoke softly, patiently.

"I won't admit that, Flint. I won't admit that because it's not true. You are good at this. Maybe not all of it, like wearing the right shoes or not drinking during the day, but you know more about this than anyone I've ever met. You're like a walking encyclopedia. But the most important thing is that, deep down, you know what the right thing is. You're not all Hollywoodland phony. There's a real man in there, who can do the right thing. I think I knew that the whole time too. If I didn't, I wouldn't have come out here with you."

"I knew that about you too. Otherwise, I wouldn't have come," Flint said. "But as for smarts, you could just replace me with any one of these."

He reached to a stack of academic textbooks that were stacked up on top of a suitcase packed tight with and grabbed one roughly off of the top, sending several books spilling to the floor. He held the volume up for Callie to see.

"I'll just leave these behind. You can parse through them and put it all together yourself, I'm sure."

"That's ridiculous. You know that's not true."

Flint sighed and shrugged. He turned to put the book back and glanced down at the ones that had fallen to the ground. He stopped in his tracks and looked down in slack-jawed surprise, frozen.

"What is it, Flint? Are you okay? Are you having a heart attack?"

He dropped the book from his hands and reached down to scoop up the new one. He held up the open page to Callie. On it was a drawing that appeared to come from the Middle Ages. It was a complicated criss-cross pattern of lines forming a cross with three middle lines. At the end of each was a circular node. All were connected by the different lined pathways so that one could trace their finger across the lines in one uninterrupted, infinite path. At the top were the words, "*The Tree of Life*."

"The Tree of Life. What is it?" Callie asked.

"It's a visual explanation for all the things that make up life. From our psyche, to God, to just everyday existence," Flint said excitedly.

He carried the book over to the small traveling desk that stood against one wall of his tent and laid the book down flat. Callie read the words in each circle: Crown, Wisdom, Mercy, Victory, Foundation, Kingdom, Beauty, Splendor, Severity, and Understanding.

"Then here we can see all the different pathways that can connect us to each one. The pathways of life," Flint continued.

He began to hurriedly root through a leather satchel, tossing out papers and pens and notebooks.

"Nobody knows exactly where the Tree of Life originated as a concept. Most likely the Assyrians in the 9th century. But Jewish mystics, the Kabbalists, utilized it in the Middle Ages. So did the Rosicrucians in the 17th century. They still do, actually. But the point is this; the Knights Templar would definitely have been well aware of it. Aha! I found it!"

He pulled a piece of paper from the satchel and hurried back to the table. He laid the paper down flat, next to the image of the Tree of Life. On the paper was a crudely drawn map representing the cross formation of the rocks that they had found out at the farmhouse.

"It's not exactly the same formation as the Tree, we're missing a few paths, but what if we laid this cross down over the Tree of Life. We still have two circular points at each end of the cross and one in the center. Remember, that was where I thought we were supposed to start digging."

Callie read the center circle. It said, "*Beauty*."

"Beauty. That sounds promising."

"Right. That's nice. But let's say that this is even a connection, right? Let's say these things do match up. That, to me, says that the Knights Templar are intentionally trying to create a situation that is difficult for someone to discover. That's obvious, we know that. *But*, with this code, it's easy for other Knights Templar to find. Otherwise, why do any of this at all? The pipes, the rocks, the carvings, all of it. Just bury whatever this treasure is so that only you know where to find it. Otherwise, it's vulnerable."

"You're rambling, McQuaid. They're gonna take the tent down around us before you're done here."

"Sorry, I'm working this out in my own head, too. Now, when you said that the Head of John the Baptist, or something like it, would be dangerous in the Nazis' hands, that makes me think…

"Maybe this isn't treasure at all. Maybe it's something terrible. Something dangerous. Something that the Knights Templar took all the way out to Oak Island centuries ago, to bury in secret, while still leaving behind an obscure key so that other Knights would be able to protect it should the time come."

"A time like this one. Where everyone is trying to find it."

"Exactly. Unfortunately for them, they're all dead now. All they have is us. Am I crazy? Does this all sound crazy?"

Flint wiped a stray hair away from his red, sweating face. He looked slightly insane, and Callie couldn't help but laugh.

"I'm not laughing because it's crazy, I promise you. This whole thing is crazy. Personally, I think you're onto something. I'll at least entertain it for the next two minutes and then you have to stop talking."

Flint took a breath, and tried to relax. He was grateful for her calming presence.

"Okay, let's see if we're both crazy together. If this was a scary, world ending object, where would you hide it in the human condition?"

Callie studied the Tree of Life. She ran her fingers along the various paths and read the words under her breath. Crown, Mercy, Victory, Foundation… Severity. She stabbed her finger at the circle containing the word.

"There. That one. It's the only option."

"I agree. That's where we should have been digging this whole time."

"Well let's saddle up and get some shovels, McQuaid."

She punched him in the shoulder and let out a little whoop.

Flint, grinning, said, "Let's just hope Weissbaum doesn't blow his wig when he finds out we promised all the Nova Scotians more money to unload all those trucks."

CHAPTER 10

Flint wedged the iron pry bar under the rock. Roy was beside him, Callie on the other side. Both had their pry bars wedged beneath the rock and angled upward, ready for them to put their weight behind.

A few of the Nova Scotians, including Dylan and John, the men who had accompanied them to the farmhouse, stood and watched. Flint was grateful that they had stuck around, not all of the work crew had, but he was annoyed none had stepped forward to move the rock when volunteers were called for. Callie could read it all over his face. She grinned at him.

"It's our mission, McQuaid. You gotta get in there and do the heavy lifting."

"Yeah, yeah. I'm doing it, aren't I? You two ready?"

Callie nodded. Roy grunted. As good as anything he was going to get. Flint counted them down and, in unison, they put all of their weight on the bars. Slowly but surely, the rock lifted up into the air. Dylan and John jumped in and helped guide the massive stone upward, until it finally tipped over on its back, revealing the entrance into a deep hole. Just wide enough for a human being to drop through.

Flint wiped his brow and spat in the dirt. "I am so tired of these damn holes and these damn rocks. If I have to move one more rock or climb in one more hole I'll go off my head."

Callie patted him on the back. "Calm down, slugger. Take a little walk, see if you can find any Nazis in the trees."

Flint snickered and paced around. Meanwhile, Dylan handed Roy a long rope, each foot demarcated on it with blue paint. A heavy weight hung on the end. Roy squatted by the edge of the hole and fed the rope down into the waiting darkness.

Callie had been joking about finding Nazis in the trees, but her stomach rose to her throat when she saw a nearby bush move. Her panic subsided when she saw a familiar head peek out. Shirley. The girl had thought she was being subtle. When she realized she was caught, she stood and waved at Callie.

"Hi Callie!" she said with a broad smile.

She popped from behind the bush and ran to Callie. Callie tried to hide her feelings when the girl hugged her tight around the waist, but she knew she was blushing. She didn't like feeling soft in front of these roughneck men, but she let the girl hug her for as long as she wanted.

When she let go and stepped back, Callie asked, "What are you doing here? Where's your mother? Don't you have supervision?"

Shirley looked up at her, confused. "Super- What? What are you asking me?"

"Nothing, never mind."

"I'm here to help you! Whatever you need me to do, I can do. I can dig. I can fight."

The fire in the girl's eyes told Callie that this was one hundred percent true.

"I know you can, Shirley. I know you can."

Roy approached, casually swinging the weight at the end of the rope.

"Hate to interrupt whatever, uh, this is. But it looks like the drop is seventeen feet. Assuming there is a corridor down there and it's not just a hole, I'm assuming that's about ten feet of earth and then seven feet of corridor space."

"Oh, that's not so bad." Callie turned to where Flint was stretching and swinging his arms like a prize fighter getting ready for the ring. "You hear that? Seventeen feet!"

"Oh, that's not so bad."

"That's what I said. Are we ready to go, Major?"

"I've already got the lines set up."

"We helped!" John called from the edge of the hole.

Roy leaned in to Callie and whispered conspiratorially, "I wouldn't tell them this, but these Canadian boys aren't so bad."

Callie knelt down in front of Shirley. She took her small hands in hers. "I have to go down into that hole. I'm sorry, but you can't follow. Those bad guys are around here. They're looking for us. They could come any moment. You have to get out of here, okay?"

"Okay. I promise."

"I know you're lying to me."

"I know."

Callie sighed and patted Shirly on the cheek.

"Please be safe, okay?"

Shirley nodded. Callie gave a start when she felt Flint's hand on her shoulder.

"You ready to find the most terrifying treasure mankind has ever seen?"

"Ready as I'll ever be," she said.

One by one, Callie, Flint, and Roy rappelled down into the hole. They'd offered extra cash to the Nova Scotians to come down with them, but even Dylan and John had refused. Apparently staying up on the surface with violent Germans on the prowl seemed like a safer deal than going into the old tunnels. Flint went down first, and he was filled with relief when his feet hit solid earth. He turned on his flashlight and clipped it to his shirt.

Moments later, Callie and Roy dropped down beside him and turned their lights on as well. The lights did their best to fight against the pitch black around them, but they weren't much. From what Flint could make out, there was a tunnel to the left and a tunnel to the right.

"I hope I get a view this good when I'm put in the ground," Callie quipped.

Flint pulled the piece of paper with the Tree of Life drawn on it from his back pocket. All three flashlights landed on it.

"So, we need to go here, to where it says Severity."

"Severity. Sounds lovely," Roy said dryly.

Flint traced the lines with his finger. "That means… we go left."

"I'm trusting you, McQuaid," Callie said.

"Thank you. I mean that."

Roy grunted, and the trio moved into the darkness.

***

Up topside, Dylan and John stood at the edge of the hole and peered down.

"Sounds like they moved on," Dylan said.

"Let's hope," John said. "Bombs away."

He kicked a clod of dirt down into the hole. They listened as it hit the ground with a satisfying thud. The two men chuckled together.

John let out a little whistle and said, "We've got some long green coming our way."

"Yessir!" Dylan elbowed his buddy in the ribs. "What're you gonna spend your bread on?"

"Top shelf hooch and a twist with legs that don't stop."

"John, they gotta stop or there's nowhere for her organs and what all to be."

"Are you an idiot?"

It took Dylan a moment to decide. He said, "Nah, I getcha. I getcha."

"If we spend too much more time around these three they'll end up using the treasure to pay for a Toronto overcoat."

Dylan shivered at the thought. "Never mind a coffin. They can cremate me. Save my family the money."

Shirley ran up and, doing her best impression of Callie, said, "You two need to quit jawing! We've got company!"

Dylan and John looked up to find gun barrels emerging from the tree line. The weapons' wielders weren't far behind. In the lead was Obersoldat Baldur Axmann, flanked by three soldiers on either side. The line of men stepped from the trees and then parted, allowing Declan and Sauer to move to the front. For a moment, the Nova Scotians and the Nazis stared at each other in silence. Then Shirley spoke up.

"You get out of here, you sons of bitches!"

Declan laughed. "My, my. She has a mouth on her, doesn't she? You probably picked that up from my brother and his odious lady friend, didn't you?"

"Shut up. Ass."

Shirley gave Declan the finger.

"We do not have time for this ballyhoo," Sauer said, irritated. He slipped his Luger P08 from the recesses of his black coat. He pointed it at John and Dylan. "Did they go down that hole?"

"Who?" Dylan asked, innocently.

"Sure did," John said. When Dylan shot him a dirty look he whispered, "I'm not getting killed for some American treasure hunters. Are you?"

Dylan shrugged. He hated the Germans, but he knew his friend was right.

"Thank you. You will die quickest," Sauer said. He waved his hand at Baldur and then another soldier. "You and you. You guard these simpletons. Do not execute them yet. The rest, you will follow me into this hole. We are going hunting."

As the men prepared to rappel down the hole, Shirley sidled up next to Baldur. She began to size him up. In her wisdom, she could tell that he didn't seem that much older than her. And he was nervous. His hands were shaking slightly.

"Hey," the little girl whispered.

He looked down at her with a deep frown.

"It's going to be okay," she said.

***

As Flint moved down the corridor, he couldn't shake the feeling that he was being watched. It was an easy thing to imagine, especially in the darkness. But he'd never had the feeling come over him as intensely as it had in that moment. He couldn't shake the vision of the man in the Money Pit. Barely alive. Groaning. Crazed. *Was he an anomaly? Were there more of him lurking in these corridors?* he wondered. Keeping his flashlight trained on the next step in front of him, he spoke to Callie and Roy.

"Do you two have a funny feeling?"

"What kind of feeling?" Callie asked. "Because I feel cold and tired and damp, but none of those are funny, so…"

"Like maybe someone is watching us right now? Or that we're being followed?"

Callie turned her flashlight back the way they'd come. Nothing.

"I think we're safe. No one's on our tail."

"I feel like we should have just blown this island up," Roy said gruffly.

Flint desperately wanted to skewer Roy back with a pithy remark, but he held it in. He needed the veteran on his side. Instead, Flint pricked his ears up. He tried to hear their boots in the soft earth, but they barely made a sound. Not a good sign if they were actually being followed. He heard water dripping. He heard insects and rodents scurrying. He heard… ragged breathing. It sounded nearly identical to the man in the Money Pit.

"Okay, that's it, there's something in here with us."

Flint stopped and the other two bumped into him.

"Ow. Dammit," Callie swore under her breath.

Roy gave him a little shove. More motivating than mean.

"We need to keep moving, boy. There's nothing down here, you're being paranoid."

Flint knew he had to finally tell them about the man he'd found in the Money Pit. He steeled himself for their looks of mocking disbelief.

"Okay, I saw something down in the Money Pit. Something was down there. I think something may be down here with us too…"

"Finally, my brother is right about something."

Flint whirled around to find Declan standing only ten feet away from them. Behind him stood Sauer and four Nazi soldiers. They looked to be spoiling for a fight.

"You should have left when you had the chance," Declan said. "This is the end, Flint. I've won. The relic is mine."

"Time for them to die," Sauer said. He sounded like a starving man ordering a cake.

"Well, hold on now," Declan sputtered. "I think their public humiliation will be enough, don't you?"

"Yeah," Flint protested quickly. "International incident. Remember, Sauer?"

“The dead stay below the earth,” Sauer murmured, seemingly to himself.

He gave an order in German to the soldiers and they raised their rifles. Flint locked eyes with Declan. If he was going to die, he wanted him to watch.

Flint said, “Half-brother. Don’t forget it.”

Then he saw something melt out of the shadows behind the soldiers. A shambling figure wielding a broadsword. He had been right the whole time. Whatever the thing in the Money Pit was, he wasn’t alone.

The man’s rotten teeth and ghoulish sunken eyes were briefly illuminated in Flint’s flashlight beam as it raised its sword above one of the young soldiers.

CHAPTER 11

The ancient Templar brought the broadsword down on the Nazi's clavicle. Perhaps the blade was deadly sharp despite its age. Perhaps the Templar's withered arms were preternaturally strong. Perhaps it was both. Whatever the cause, the sword cut through the soldier like butter, slashing through his shoulder, down his ribcage, and ending in his stomach. The soldier didn't even have time to scream. He was dead before he hit the ground.

Everyone else had enough time to scream, though.

United by an outside threat, the Nazis and the explorers ignored each other and turned their flashlights down the corridor to find the Templar covered in the soldier's blood and raising his sword for another swing at whoever was closest. But that wasn't all. Behind him, barely illuminated in the collection of flashlight beams, were more than a dozen half-dead knights.

They wore tattered clothing and rusted chain mail. Their helmets sat lopsided on their aging heads. But with swords and pikes and crossbows, they were terrifying. Their sunken yellow eyes were alive with rage. Crazed, even. They were hungry for violence. Desperate for blood.

Instantly, everything erupted in chaos. Guns roared. Blades slashed.

Flint didn't have a plan, but he knew he had to do something. Anything, really. He did the smartest thing he could think of.

"Run!" he yelled to Callie.

He grabbed her by the hand and pulled her along with him. She didn't have to be asked twice. She pulled her knees up and matched his pace, following down the corridor, away from the noise. Away from the violence and the blood.

They ran until all those things were a distant sound. They stopped for a moment to catch their breath.

"It seems like a sidenote in all this chaos, but where exactly are we going?" Callie asked in between puffs.

"Severity, remember?" Flint held up the map. He gestured with his flashlight. "If we keep going this way, we'll find it."

"I don't know if going deeper into this hellhole is the best idea."

Flint cocked his head and listened. Callie followed suit. They heard a sound coming toward them. Slow, staggering footfalls and a dragging noise, as if someone was pulling something behind them. A body, perhaps?

"Well, we can't go back that way," Flint said. "We have to go deeper."

As they hurried down the filthy tunnel, a thought occurred to Callie.

"Say, where the devil is Roy?"

***

Major Jake Roy wasn't scared. He didn't get scared. Not anymore. He was, however, wired hot. Full of adrenaline. A deep need to survive. He told himself that wasn't fear. He wasn't a psychologist, but for all he knew he was right. It made him feel better, even as he was standing there at the dead-end of an underground tunnel being pursued by monsters and Nazis.

There has to be a way out, he thought. *There just has to be. I didn't survive all I did just to die in goddamn Canada.*

With the sharp, tight beam of his flashlight, he ran his hands over the dirt walls seeking some sort of seam. Any point of weakness that he could exploit. They hadn't dropped that far down. Only ten feet to the surface. He could tunnel through ten feet.

His hands found a patch of rocks. A wide cluster of stones that had fallen together centuries ago to create a vein cutting through the dirt. He peered through the mass and saw a thin ribbon of sunlight eking through.

Sunlight. Life.

Before he could start digging, he heard screams and gunshots echoing down a connecting corridor. Roy didn't know who was still alive and who wasn't. He hoped Flint and Callie were okay. He couldn't blame them for getting away as fast as they could. After all, he'd been hired to protect them, not the other way around.

After they took off, he'd taken a few precise shots and blown his way out of there. He'd taken one of those living dead knight's heads clean off. He'd been almost as surprised to see it could die as he was to see it alive.

The sounds were getting closer.

He pulled his revolver from his belt and flicked the cylinder open. Click. Just as he thought. Every cartridge was spent. He dumped them out into the dirt at his feet and fingered out more from his pocket. He was about to start loading them in when he heard footsteps sprinting his way and a voice that was swearing in German. He couldn't make out who it was, but a flashlight was bobbing up and down and getting nearer with every step.

As fast as he was, Roy wouldn't be able to load up in time. He turned his back to the oncoming flashlight and slid a bullet up under his eyepatch. He felt it nestle down into his eye socket, hidden to the world. When he turned around he found Sauer standing in front of him, panting.

In one hand he clutched a flashlight. In the other, his Luger.

The sour little man shone the light in Roy's face and grinned. "Oh, it's you."

"Shoulda known I was gonna see you again, you creepy little Kraut." Roy spat at the Nazi's feet.

Sauer laughed. "I suppose I should have killed you when I last had the opportunity. But now it will be sweeter. My desire for your blood has been rising, and now I can savor the moment."

He licked his lips as if he were contemplating eating a fine steak, then trained his gun on Roy.

"Drop the pistol, please. And the bullets."

"Yeah, yeah, I'll drop *ze* bullets."

He let them all fall to the ground. He clipped his flashlight to his shirt pocket and put his hands on his head. He knew the drill. In the eerie light, Sauer's pale white face looked hollow and ghostly. His ever-present grin was ghastlier than ever.

"You may think that I do what I do simply to fulfill some sort of strange pleasure. You do, don't you?"

Roy didn't answer. He was more concerned with figuring out what to do with the bullet in his eye socket. He wouldn't be able to grab the revolver from the dirt and load it in time… He remembered an anecdote that Weissbaum had told him once. *Fucking Weissbaum.* In the story, a British soldier had taken out a German by throwing a bullet at a rock. It had hit the primer with just enough speed and force to ignite the powder and fire the lead right between the guy's eyes. He hadn't believed it at the time, but now he felt like he had to.

Sauer continued. "I do what I do, the way that I do it, because of principles. Very specific principles that mean something dear to me."

Roy began to edge his hand down to his eyepatch. He just needed to keep Sauer distracted and talking.

"Lemme guess. A bunch of Nazi bullshit, right?"

"Well, I wouldn't put it that way, but… yes."

With a quick movement of his left hand, Roy flipped the eyepatch up. The bullet tumbled from his socket, and he caught it in his right. He threw the bullet as hard and as fast as he could at a jagged, pointed rock jutting from the dirt wall just a couple feet away from Sauer's head, and he prayed.

It didn't work.

It did, however, rebound off of the rock and ping against Sauer's forehead.

"Ah, what in the blazes?"

He swatted at the bullet and turned away for a split second. That was all Roy needed. He was immediately upon Sauer, struggling over the Luger. He was bigger and stronger than the German, and it didn't take long for him to knock the gun from the Nazi's hand and kick it away.

Roy stepped back and said, "Hand to hand, Sauer. Let's go."

"Yes. Fine. That is fair."

With that, Sauer reached into his long, black coat and pulled out an onyx-handled knife. He flipped it open, revealing a gleaming blade. He slashed at Roy, first to the right, then to the left. Roy dodged each attack, jumping backwards until his back hit the wall.

"Now you are trapped. Like an American dog."

Sauer advanced upon him, knife at the ready.

Roy dug his hand into the dirt wall and came away with a fistful of earth. He flung the soil into Sauer's face, blinding him. Roy knocked the knife out of the whimpering German's hand. He grabbed him by the back of the head. With all his might, he swung Sauer's face into the pointed end of the rock that had once been part of his bullet plan. He knew it was done after one hit, but he brought his head down twice more before dropping Sauer's body to the ground. It brought Roy no pleasure, but he'd learned in the past that it was better to be safe than sorry.

There was a moment of creeping silence after the life left Sauer. Roy stood there in the inky black corridor with the dead body. He breathed a sigh of relief. He wasn't scared. He was grateful to be alive.

Then he heard the scampering feet and weird grunts of the ancient Templars reverberating down the corridors. For the second time, death was coming closer and closer.

He picked up Sauer's Luger and dusted it off. He squared his shoulders and steeled himself for a fight that he hoped wouldn't be his last.

***

Callie and Flint came to a stop. They couldn't hear any fighting or footfalls. It seemed they were as safe as they could be. Their path had led them along several crisscrossing corridors, all sloping downward. Now they were at a crossroads, an X-shaped intersection, where four different paths came together and then broke apart again.

"I'm pretty sure Severity is this way…" he checked the map again. "I might have gotten a bit turned around, what with all the living Templar knights and all. We may have gotten turned around at that last juncture…"

"I really don't want to be buried alive. At least not until I make my movie."

"Our movie."

"That's right. Our movie."

A flashlight beam suddenly hit them in the eyes and they both jumped back in fear. They turned their own lights to find Declan standing in front of them. His eyes were wide with shock. His face was covered in spattered blood. His mouth kept opening and closing like a dying fish. A weird, guttural sound came out each time.

"Declan, Jesus!" Flint hissed at him in the dark.

"I didn't even hear you coming," Callie said.

"He's not wearing any shoes."

Flint tilted his flashlight down to show Callie Declan's filthy, stockinged feet.

"I-I-I-I took them o-off," Declan stuttered. "Threw them at the m-m-monsters."

Flint stepped closer to Declan, who shied away from him. He persisted and put his hand on his brother's shoulder. Declan's whole body was trembling beneath his touch.

"Are you okay?" Flint asked, lamely. The answer was obvious, but he didn't know what else to say to the brother he barely knew.

Declan shook his head in quick little jerks.

"Th-the Templar took the s-s-sword and cleaved it right into the sol-, uh, the soldier's he-head. I s-s-s-saw his brains."

He drew the word 'brains' out for a long beat and his voice began to catch as if he were about to cry, but no tears came out. His eyes just remained wide as dinner plates.

"How did you find us?" Carrie asked.

"Wasn't l-l-looking for you. I was going to Severity…"

His speech drifted away, and a faraway look overtook his face.

He was looking for Severity too, Flint thought. *Great minds think alike. Or good minds, at least.*

Looking at his half-brother then, shocked and traumatized, Flint realized that they were both following the same North Star: Their father. For all of Declan's faults, and they were many, they were imprinted by a man who had treated both of them with disdain. Still, Flint decided, Declan had made his own bed, regardless of who had taught him to make it.

Then the ground fell out from under them and the three of them were tumbling through darkness.

***

They landed on the hard, tightly packed earth. Flint felt the wind get knocked out of him. He took a moment to catch his breath and stood up, aiming his flashlight around the pitch-black space they now found themselves. It took him a moment to realize that there was only one beam of light.

"Turn your light on, genius," Flint said to Callie.

She held up her flashlight. The glass lens was shattered, along with the bulb.

"It's broken, genius."

"Damn. Declan, what about you?"

Declan was staring, dead-eyed, down at the ground and fluttering his fingers.

"It didn't uh, didn't make it d-d-down here."

"You dropped it? Are you kidding me? Dammit! I thought you were supposed to be the genius, but you can't even hold onto a flashlight. I swear to God, Declan…"

Flint waved the flashlight around their new surroundings. As he expected, it was a tight fit. A perfectly cut cube in the earth. As opposed to the moist, uneven surfaces of the corridors, littered with rocks and roots and insects, the walls of the cube were packed tightly. They were perfectly flat and dry, with no sign of life. Strange, but Flint was too enraged to take much notice.

"Oh *great*, another tiny little hole. You know what? I'm gonna get us out of here, and you know why? Because I got myself out the exact same jam when you and the old man cut me loose and left me there to die in Egypt! I got out, Declan! I survived and I made a life for myself without you or that cruel old son of a bitch. And I'll do the same thing now, despite the fact that I *loathe* you. Because I am the good brother, you crumb! You lout! I am the good one."

He realized he'd been yelling and clammed up, embarrassed at losing control.

"Oh, Flint…" Callie's voice murmured in the dark.

He turned his flashlight on Callie. She was looking at him, a deep sadness consuming her expression.

He opened his mouth to explain, but a loud, sudden buzzing filled his head like radio static. He wasn't alone. Callie and Declan both covered their ears, but it did no good. The sound was so overpowering that they all began to instinctively collapse, dropping to their knees.

"Why isn't it getting quieter when I cover my ears?" Callie yelled.

"I think it's playing in our heads," Flint said through gritted teeth.

Then, just as suddenly, a voice began to play in Flint's brain. It replaced the static completely. The voice was weak. A ghostly rasp.

What do you choose? the voice asked telepathically. *Your brother's life? Or the relic?*

"Do you hear that? It's like a ghost talking in my brain."

Despite her pain, Callie raised a confused eyebrow at him. Even Declan looked at him like he was crazy.

Once again, the voice asked: *What do you choose? Your brother's life? Or the relic?*

Flint's thoughts flew by faster than the frames of a movie reel. Images from his life. He and his brother as boys. The spineless Nazi cooperator that stood before him now. Flint holding the head of John the Baptist. Appearing on the covers of magazines. Riches. Fame. Then he saw Declan lying in a coffin. It was too much for him to bear. He knew then. It had to be Declan.

Declan. I choose my brother's life! he thought as fervently as he could.

After a long moment of silence, the ghostly voice replied, *I am not sure that I believe you.*

The static stopped and Callie and Declan slowly rose to their feet. Both were disoriented and still clearly in some pain.

"Whatever that thing was, I hope it believes me."

"What in the hell are you talking about, McQuaid?" Callie wriggled a finger in her ear.

Flint didn't need to reply. The answer came when one of the walls began to move toward them. It moved slowly along the perfectly level ground. There was no way out. They were going to be crushed like bugs.

CHAPTER 12

"What the-? Why is the wall moving?!" Callie hollered.

"It asked me a question telepathically. It was a moral question. A test."

"Oh, aces! You, and a test of morality? I'm sure we'll be just dandy then!" her voice was dripping sarcasm.

Flint dropped his flashlight to the ground, casting an eerie spotlight against Declan, who was shuddering and muttering to himself. Unencumbered, Flint threw himself against the wall as it enclosed upon them. He dug his heels into the dirt, but the stone panel kept advancing.

"Passing a moral test doesn't mean you don't get your teeth kicked in anyway," Flint said through gritted teeth and grunts of effort against the moving wall.

"Oh, how the hell would you know?" Callie snapped.

Flint ignored her and shouted over his shoulder to Declan. "Can you pull your head out of your ass and help me here?"

He glanced back to find that Declan was standing stock still, his hands stuck out like trembling claws, and he stared down at the ground as he mumbled to himself.

"Aw, dammit," Flint swore bitterly. He wanted to hate his brother for his inaction, but now he just felt sorry for him. He regretted the bile he had spewed at him only moments before. Sure, in all the years since they'd last spoken, he hadn't held a single kind word for his brother. But now, seeing how weak he was, how spineless, Flint truly did want only to help him. He hoped whatever entity had been speaking to him understood that.

But there wasn't time for hoping. A wall was slowly moving in on them with the sole purpose of turning them into crepes. Flint threw himself back against the wall and pushed as hard as he could.

"I don't like tight spaces! I don't like tight spaces!" He hollered it in a panic, no thought at all behind it, and was embarrassed to have exposed himself like that in front of Callie.

He tried as hard as he could to hold the wall, but he couldn't even slow it. He knew it was useless.

He looked to Callie with an expression that roughly translated to "*Help me!*" only to find that she was giving him the exact same one. Their looks quickly faded into wry smiles. *Nothing to help with...*

"I'm trying to let a sense of calm wash over me. They say that happens when you're about to be crushed to death in Canada," Callie said.

"Let's hope so," Flint said. He sighed. Maybe it was his destiny to die in a dark tomb after all. All the running in the world couldn't keep him from becoming who he was meant to become. "By the way, Callie, I… Before we go, I might as well tell you-"

Then the overwhelming grinding sound ceased. The approaching wall had stopped, frozen in place.

Could the voice have reconsidered? Flint wondered.

"Oh, thank God." Callie let out a sigh of relief. "I did not have a sense of calm."

Flint forced a laugh. "Yeah, me neither."

Declan mumbled something that made it sound as if he were glad to be alive.

The trio watched as the wall in front of them slowly retracted to the right. Loose clumps of soil fell away, and vines broke, filling the tiny space with enough dust to start them all choking. Then the wall was gone, vanished into the earth, as if by magic.

In its place stood a narrow staircase carved into the earth. Flint retrieved his flashlight and shone it up the stairwell. The stairs were slick with moisture and crawling with bugs. Rocks dotted their surface. It looked treacherous, at best.

"Severity…" Declan whispered.

Callie looked from the stairs to Flint. "So… Whoever these guys are, I think they want us to go up?"

"Looks like it." Flint snapped his fingers and got Declan's attention. "Declan, let's go find this relic."

***

Five minutes of climbing later, the three of them emerged from the staircase into a musty, dank space. Torches dotted the walls, filling the room with a faint, flickering glow. The flames were a strange, green color, unlike anything Flint had seen before. Still, he was relieved that the room was big enough to breathe in.

Callie rubbed her eyes and tried to focus on the dim room. "How are the torches going? Is there oxygen in this room?"

"I don't know if we're following the laws of nature here," Flint said.

He shone his flashlight around the room, finding what details he could. The floor, walls, and ceiling were all naked earth. Roots broke through the surfaces. The ceiling dripped murky water and churned with earthworms. Stick-thin wooden furniture was scattered about. A couple of chairs. A small table. A bed. Its straw mattress had long since rotted away.

The edges of the room fell away in shadow, making it impossible to tell exactly how large the room was. Or what was in it.

He froze when his light fell on something in the very center of the room. It sat on a stone pedestal carved with the same runes that they had discovered on the stone markings up above. It was covered in a heavy glass dome. A light emanated from inside, though it was impossible to tell what was generating it.

"Is that? No…" Callie's voice fell away in shock.

"It's impossible," Flint said.

When Declan saw it he gasped, then let out a little squeak of demented pleasure. He shuffled toward the object like some kind of mindless Igor. Flint hurried to him and, grabbing him by the shoulder, pulled him backwards. Declan fell to the ground and whimpered in protest but stayed where he lay.

Flint and Callie slowly approached the pedestal. They crouched down to get a better look at the object and came face to face with a severed head, bathed in a ghostly glow. The olive brown skin hadn't aged a day over thirty. The dark brown hair and beard were clean and in place. The closed eyes seemed at peace. The lips were turned upward into a subtle, beatific grin.

"Jesus Christ. It's the head of John the Baptist," Flint muttered.

"Don't take the Lord's name in vain in front of… that," Callie scolded him.

Once they spoke, the head's eyelids snapped open. The eyes were clear and so alert that they were almost manic. They darted around the room as if looking for the source of the sound, but never settled on Callie and Flint.

"Can he hear us?" Callie asked.

"Let's find out."

Flint raised his hand to tap against the glass dome.

A choked, raspy voice came from the shadows.

"Please. Do not percuss the glass."

They turned to find a man so thin, so desiccated, that he resembled a corpse more than a man. But his blinking yellow eyes proved him to be alive. He wore black leggings and matching tunic. They were so decayed they were practically rags, but Flint could still make out the large red cross sewn onto the tunic. Another Templar.

Flint searched about for a weapon and settled on a fist-sized stone resting in the dirt nearby. He raised the stone above his head in the most threatening way he could muster.

"Please, young man. Calm yourself."

He spoke haltingly, in a lilting French accent. *It would be charming if he didn't look so ghastly*, Callie thought.

Flint raised the rock higher. "Calm myself?! Your noble goons were out there ventilating everyone in sight with their rusty broadswords."

"Yes. They have been driven mad."

"And what about you?" Callie asked, stepping forward, her hands tightened into meaty fists.

"Myself? Am I mad?" the man asked in reply.

The question hung in the air for a moment before Callie realized it wasn't rhetorical.

"Right. Are you mad?" she said.

"Oh yes so, I believe I am. Very perceptive of you, thank you for asking. Impossible to tell after having been alive this long, but I do not believe I am the man who crawled down here. No, I have been broken very well by time."

Flint lowered the rock, but he didn't drop it.

He asked, "What's your name? Who are you?"

The old man shuffled over to one of the spindly wooden chairs. He flicked a crawling beetle off of its armrest and slowly, delicately, sat down in it. It creaked even under his slight weight. The Templar sighed. To Flint, he seemed so deflated compared to his vicious compatriots, as if he didn't possess their strength at all. Whether that was a result of being isolated in the chamber or a simple lack of will, Flint couldn't tell. The old man spoke.

"I do not recall my name. Isn't that funny?" He wheezed out a little giggle between his dry, thin lips. "That is funny."

"Yeah, it's hilarious. You're a real Ben Turpin. What the hell is going on here, old man?"

"I remember… I remember I was once the Commander of the Vault of Acre. A hallowed role in the Knights Templar," the old man began, ploddingly. "We came here, oh… early in the 13th… it was 1312. Yes, that was it. How I remember that and not my own name… Strange."

"1312. The same year Pope Clement V ended the Templars," Flint said quietly.

"Very good, young man. You are an intelligent group. When they began to hunt down the brotherhood that we had created, we knew that we had artifacts with power beyond those fools' understanding. We knew that they could not fall into the wrong hands.

"The most powerful amongst them was the head of John the Baptist. His gifts are too great for the weak or the power hungry.

"And so, we took the relic here. We created this underground lair. We swore to live here, beneath the earth, silently waiting to fight against all who may seek to take him and use his power to control others.

"It is his power that has kept us alive all these centuries. His power that keeps these torches burning and our lungs breathing this stale, fetid air. His power that allows me to see above the surface, to witness the awful decline of mankind.

"We left encoded messages on the rocks, signals to surviving Templars or future believers who may come to relieve us of our duty but… none came."

“Maybe you shouldn’t have left road signs all over the island,” Flint offered, helpfully.

“Wait, hold on,” Callie said in a near whisper. “Through him you can… see the world above the surface?”

Flint almost snickered seeing Callie dumbfounded. He never thought he’d see her lost in awe.

“Yes. He is a roaming set of eyes and ears. Through direct contact with him I am able to fly above the land to any point on the globe. I have watched empires rise and fall from this humble little hole. All the while waiting for someone like you, of course.”

Flint interjected. “Direct contact? You touch that thing?”

Before the old man could reply, the trio heard the clinking of glass on stone. They turned to find Declan kneeling by the stone pillar. He was desperately trying to remove the glass globe to gain access to the head. The head’s eyes were darting wildly. Its brows were furrowed, its lips were creased into a hard frown. John the Baptist was angry.

So was the old man.

“Stop him! Stop that creature!”

Flint hesitated for only a second. By the time he started moving, Callie was already on Declan, grabbing him from behind in a wrestling hold. Like lightning, she had her arms wrapped around his shoulders and her hands clenched together behind his head. He kicked his feet and waved his arms like a limp ragdoll. He cried out angrily, spittle flying from his lips.

“Get him, Flint! Get him! It’s why we’re here! It’s why we’ve done everything our whole lives!”

Then he was grunting and gasping as Callie threw her arm around his neck and tightened his neck between her bicep and forearm.

"Dammit, he's going limp!" Callie said through gritted teeth.

Declan kept babbling histrionically through his ever-tightening windpipe.

"Shut your yap or I'll make you pass out."

With that, Declan quieted.

"That woman behaves as a man," the Templar murmured. His tone was a mix of shock and admiration.

"She's got it under control," Flint said.

He gave Callie a grateful smile. As much as he loathed his half-brother, his hesitation had proven that he didn't actually want to hurt him. Callie stepping up had saved him from that. She gave him a wink, a sign of reassurance, a sign that she knew exactly where he was at.

"Just ignore him," Flint said. "What were you talking about?"

"I… I have no idea…" the old man said. Then he stood up as if hit with a sudden jolt of electricity. "How long have you been here? How long have we been talking here?"

"About twenty minutes, I think," Callie said, then added, "You were talking about how you can see through John the Baptist's eyes."

"Oh yes, that was it! Empires rising and falling and all that," Flint said.

"That's right…" the old man began pacing around the musty room. "I have seen the great evils that man has concocted. I see the storm brewing in Europe now. I fear it will overtake my home, France. I fear it will overtake the whole world. Men are malleable. Selfish. Few are truly evil independently, but it takes very little for them to be swayed by the ones who are.

"Further, I have seen the weapons of war that man has created. Armaments that spew fire and projectiles.

Great machines dedicated to destruction. Noxious gasses that destroy all that they come into contact with. Moving images of propaganda.

"Seeing these things, they tell me that our ways of war are over. Our rusting swords are no match for your machines. Further, these visions, they… they fill me with regret. My warring years seem so far away, yet they are the clearest memories I have. Now I see we fought, we died, we *killed* for nothing. The world keeps going. The lust for power never leaves."

As if the very idea was sapping the last of his lifeforce, the old man slumped back down into the chair. For a long moment he stared at the ground in silence. Finally, he spoke.

"We hid the relic away because we believed that man would evolve. Become better, smarter. Kinder. We believed that this great power could then be brought to the surface and used for good.

"I know that this is impossible. I know that humanity is brutal and selfish. Perhaps us Templars most of all.

"The men you met in the catacombs, they refuse to accept this. They stay committed to fighting to protect our relic for the future. Meanwhile, I have waited for someone like you to come. I have accepted that evil will conquer."

"Wait, why Nova Scotia?" Callie asked.

The old man considered this, idly chewing at his thin, cracked bottom lip. "I… I do not recall that either. Isn't that funny?"

Flint moved to sit in the other chair, to get down on the Templar's level. As soon as he tested his weight in the old chair's seat he thought better of it and crouched. He looked the old man dead in his eyes. He tried his absolute best to come across as sincere. To shed the arrogant, Hollywoodland attitude that he had used as a defense mechanism for so long.

"What if…" Flint spoke, measured and quiet. "What if I told you that we're here to relieve you. We want to keep the relic from evil."

Suddenly, Declan burst out yelling.

"Wait! Flint, no! Imagine what the world would say if we could deliver this to the archeological community. The money. The respect. The women. Imagine what *Father* would say. Imagine how proud of us he would be. How proud of *you* he would be."

His father's pride. A feeling he'd never experienced. A feeling he had wanted his entire life. The words hit Flint harder than any punch he'd ever taken. He tried to continue, but for a moment, his plea caught in his throat.

"Flint…" Callie began but trailed off.

She didn't have to continue. Her message was clear: *Do the right thing.* He cleared his throat and spoke to the old man.

"Sir, believe us. We are good people. We are here to keep it from the hands of very, very bad men. The war machine you were describing but… even worse, I believe."

It was only then that Flint realized that he didn't have to fake sincerity. He *was* sincere.

The old man leaned back in his chair and assessed Flint with a bemused smile.

"Ah, yes? You seek to keep it from the hands of evil men? And why should I believe you are the benevolent ones?"

Frustration with the elderly overtook his aching sincerity and Flint blurted out, "Aw, come on, pally! Didn't I just pass your little morality test back there?"

The man let out a dry chuckle. He said, "For most men, morality lives only in the moment. And forgive me, but John and I are sensing that perhaps you are not the most selfless man."

Flint considered this. He knew the old man was right.

"I'm not. But I'm trying. I think even a nineteen-hundred-year-old head could see that. I swear to you, we don't want to keep the relic. We want to…" He couldn't believe what he was about to say. "We want to destroy it."

Slowly, the old man rose from his chair. He ambled over to the head of John the Baptist. With surprising dexterity, he carefully lifted the heavy glass dome from off of the man's head. The glow that mysteriously emanated from him did not abate. Somehow, he was even more awe-inspiring and shocking to see when the glass was removed. Callie and Declan, still entwined in a constricting embrace, stared with mouths and eyes agape.

In the expeditions he had ventured out in, all the wonders he had beheld, nothing made Flint feel the way the relic did. A mix of terror and joy. A near mania. He immediately regretted vowing to destroy what was left of John the Baptist. He fought the feeling back down.

The ancient Templar lowered himself down on his knees before the head. His joints cracked loudly and echoed through the room. He lovingly placed both of his withered hands on either side of John, almost as if he were caressing the face of a lover. He leaned in until his forehead rested against John's. He looked into John's eyes. Not a sound filled the room. The old man's tired eyes grew wider and wider. His breath quickened. He smiled.

He pulled away from John, looked at Callie, then Flint, and said, "You are telling the truth. We are both ready to meet God face to face."

"Thank you," Flint said. "How do we destroy… that?"

"You are obviously familiar with the Tree of Life, yes? Of course, that is how you found us. Go to the spot marked 'Mercy' on the Tree map. Buried deep beneath the rock there is a hidden dam. That dam is the only thing interrupting an irrigation system leading from the nearby cove to these catacombs."

"That's what those weird pipes we found when we got here are for!" Callie said, more to herself than anyone else.

"It is a final act of destruction," the old man said. "A final act to rend the head of its life force and to hide away the artifact once and for all. To ensure that none will find it again. If you destroy the dam, the catacombs will flood and collapse, entombing the relic and killing us all, including John." A small grin played upon his lips. "How can I remember all this and yet not recall my own name?"

"Come with us," Callie implored. "The wisdom you have, the stories you could tell from centuries ago. Your change of heart, if people could see it, might help make humanity a little bit better. Like you had all hoped."

The old man let out a wistful sigh.

"I wish I could see the surface one more time. But I swore to stay with John no matter the consequences. I promised to meet my end with him. We will face God together. Now, let us go. I will take you to the exit."

CHAPTER 13

One of the positives of setting up their camp so close to the cove was that Flint was able to sprint there and back to get the explosives needed to destroy the dam. He had never imagined that that would be such a plus, but there he was. Doubled over and winded with a pile of dynamite and a plunger in his hands.

"My God, you sound like you just smoked a carton of Chesterfields," Callie said, as she wiped her dirty hands on her pants.

"I was running for my life out there."

"Well in the time it took you to get there and back I cleared not one, but two, rocks."

"Two?"

For the first time, Flint took in their surroundings. The earth was soft and moist from the cove water leaching inland. Not quite swampy but given time he could imagine it becoming a marshland. They were surrounded by tall grass and reeds, obscuring the ground completely unless you were standing right over it. It was the perfect place to hide something as sensitive as the dam.

Declan was pacing around a spot about ten feet away from where Flint was catching his breath. He couldn't tell what his brother was looking at, but the man was staring at a spot in the ground and mumbling to himself.

"That's right, two. See where he is, acting like Robert Montgomery in *Riptide*? That's another hole leading down into the catacombs. I guess they wanted an entrance point near the cove that bypassed the dam. I uncovered that one first. Then, two feet to your left?"

She pointed and Flint followed her instructions. He took exactly two steps to the left and found an open hole with a large, filthy rock shoved to the side. This hole was smaller, a bit too snug for a human to comfortably pass through and it didn't lead downward. It was shallow, Flint estimated it to be about four feet deep. Enough for water to comfortably run through. Inside was the rudimentary, medieval dam. It consisted of four layers of wooden slats, built from what appeared to be the hull planks of a boat. They had been sealed together with thick black pitch to protect against leakage and decay. In between each slat was a layer of tightly packed earth and rock.

It had stood firm for hundreds of years. A testament to the ingenuity and hard work of the Templars. Now Flint was going to blow it up.

He turned to Callie. "Ready to set off this bottle rocket?"

"More than you know," she replied.

Flint dropped to his knees beside the dam and began to place the dynamite as strategically as he knew how to. He wasn't a demolitions expert, but he knew enough to know that the six sticks he had entwined together and leading to the plunger, were enough to tear apart the old wood and dirt. He was placing the last stick when Declan cried out.

"Please! Flint, don't do this!"

Flint looked up to find his brother still hovering around the second hole. For the first time since the Templar attack he seemed lucid, if a bit manic.

With wide, excited eyes, he yelled, "Think of the significance! I'm begging you. Father is begging you. I know we've had differences in the past, but this is bigger than that. Even bigger than Father. This discovery will change the world!"

Flint ignored his brother. Forget him. Forget their father. Sending John the Baptist to his final resting place would change the world as well.

As Flint backed away from the hole, carefully leading the explosive line, he felt at peace. Maybe he hadn't been destined to die in a dark tomb, he decided. Maybe he was destined to do something greater. To help people in whatever way he could manage. He hoped that was true. It was, at the very least, a lot better than the alternative.

"Please!" Declan cried again, with a fervor that almost frightened Flint.

Flint stopped, fifty feet away from the hole. He set the box with the detonation plunger in it on the ground. He visually checked in with Callie and found that she had already cleared the distance herself. Declan, however, was still standing over the second hole.

Declan continued, "We're not *that* different. Half-brothers be damned. We're united by Father. We are brothers. I know you don't want to do this."

"I don't want to. I *have* to. Now back away from the hole, Declan. I'm gonna blow this thing sky high."

Declan began to back away, but he kept his eyes on the second hole. He looked like he was planning something. What it was, Flint couldn't tell. At this point, there was no going back. What Declan could hope to accomplish was a mystery.

Flint gripped both sides of the plunger tightly. He waited until Declan had put ten more feet between himself and the dam. Flint estimated that at that distance he would probably just get hit with some clods of earth and an errant rock or two, which is what he deserved. A stone to the head might knock some sense into him. Flint looked from Callie to Declan, registering his intent with both of them. *The dam is going up.*

"I'm going to count down," he called. "3… 2…"

Flint couldn't hear himself say "1" over the sound of Declan yelling out, "I know you won't do it!" before running toward the second hole.

But Declan was wrong. Flint had already begun depressing the plunger. It was too late. There was no going back.

Flint watched in horror as Declan sprinted toward the second hole and leapt in, feet first. He disappeared beneath the surface of the earth just as Flint completed pushing down the plunger.

A few seconds later the explosion went off. Soil and smoke filled the air. Bits of pitch-covered wood and rocky insulation rained down around Callie and Flint. The dam had been decimated. In its place, there was a small crater. Cove water immediately began flowing freely, following the tunnel system down into the catacombs.

Flint ran to the second hole and dropped to his knees beside it. He peered down into it but saw only rushing water in the shadowy space. He called Declan's name again and again, even though he knew it was pointless. He didn't stop until he felt Callie's hand on his shoulder.

He looked up to find her sympathetic eyes gazing down at him.

"I'm sorry, Flint. I don't think we can get him out of there."

He knew she was right. She helped him to his feet. He started brushing the dirt off of his pants until he realized he was completely covered in a fine layer of it. He pulled a silk handkerchief from his back pocket. He wiped the sweat from his brow. He dabbed at the tears forming in the corners of his eyes.

"You don't have to hide that," Callie said to him. "But you might want to clean your mustache up a little bit."

Despite his pain, he smiled. He handed her the handkerchief. She spat on it and wiped the dirt from her face. Her bright red hair was dulled with dust, but Flint still found her, in that moment, beautiful nonetheless. When he caught her chuckling softly to herself he asked, "What's so funny?"

"Oh, nothing really. It's just after all this you still had a clean silk hankie in your pocket. You're nothing if not consistent, McQuaid."

"I'll take that as a compliment."

"It is."

She tossed the handkerchief back to him and began walking back to where they had begun. Back to where the Nazis were holding their Canadian friends hostage. Flint followed.

***

When Flint and Callie arrived back at the site, they found Dylan, John, and Shirley all standing around the hole. No Nazis to be seen. The rest of the Nova Scotians had disappeared as well. The three of them looked like they had lost their parents at the circus and didn't know exactly what to do so they had stayed in the last spot they'd seen them.

As they approached, Shirley ran up and gave Callie a hug that stopped her in her tracks. It warmed Flint to see that there was some love coming out of this event. For a moment an image of Declan trapped beneath the earth with the Templars flashed in his mind. He pushed it out.

John and Dylan waved at them, a bit sheepishly. Flint waved back.

Callie patted Shirley on the head. "Shirley, what happened here? Where did the bad men go?"

"There was one man. He was young. Younger than him, for sure." Shirley pointed at Flint. "He seemed nervous. I talked to him for a bit and eventually he let us go. He told the other men to lower their guns and they all just walked away into the woods."

"That's amazing, Shirley. Good job. I'm so proud of you."

The little girl beamed.

A nervous young man? Flint grinned and murmured, to himself, "Obersoldat Baldur Axmann…"

"Huh? Who? That sounds familiar," Callie said.

"Oh, nothing. Never mind." He turned to John and Dylan. "What are you boys still doing here?"

"We're uh, well, we wanted to make sure we were still going to get paid," John said.

"And we wanted to see how it was all going to end," Dylan said.

"Yeah, we were a bit curious about that."

"Well, I guess you got a happy ending," Flint said.

Callie knelt down in front of Shirley and brushed the girl's wild locks from her face.

"I'm going to give you my address in California. You better write to me, do you understand?"

The girl broke into a wide smile and nodded.

Flint saw someone, or something, approaching them in the distance. He shielded his eyes from the sun and squinted at the figure.

He said, "Well, well. Nothing can kill that one-eyed piece of leather, can it?"

Callie followed his gaze and watched as Roy walked toward them. The soldier was covered in dirt and grime. He had a bit of a limp, as if he'd twisted an ankle. Callie walked up next to Flint and threw her arm around his shoulders. She waved at Roy, and he raised a hand in greeting.

“How do you think the movie will end, Callie?” Flint spoke softly. Callie could hear the mix of hope and sadness in his voice.

“I don’t know yet,” she said gently. “Happily, I think.”

EPILOGUE

Callie stared up at the clear blue California sky. There, in the protected little oasis of Hollywoodland, all of the action of Oak Island seemed like it had never happened. The fact that she now considered Flint McQuaid a friend and was floating in his pool was undeniable proof that it had. Well, that and the fact that their movie was about to be released.

She rolled off of the floating bed and plunged into the water. Holding her breath, she sank down to the bottom of the pool. It occurred to her that it was the first time in a very long time that she had had a moment of quiet to herself. Since they'd arrived back it had been nothing but development meetings, film production days, and press interviews. She opened her eyes and studied her bikini-clad body, the way the colorful images on her arms seemed to dance underwater as the shimmering sun hit them. She smiled.

When she floated to the top and broke the surface, she found Flint standing at the edge of the pool wearing nothing but his swim trunks with a big cardboard tube in his hand.

"You won't believe it!" he said, smiling bigger than she'd ever seen.

"What, did your enormous pleasure tool come in the mail?"

"That's a good one, but no. The test printing for our poster came in today."

He reached into the tube and removed a sheet of glossy, rolled up paper. He unfurled it and held it up for her to see. In the center were two actors made to look like Flint and Callie. All around them, the illustrator had drawn the acting doppelgangers of Maj. Roy, Sauer, Declan, and Shirley. Callie had really made the little girl a supporting heroine in her screenplay version of their adventure. The images promised action, excitement, intrigue. Everything that audiences craved. At the bottom was the title, in big bold font: The Oak Island Enigma. Callie had to admit, it looked fantastic.

"Oh, Flint. I love it. But those actors, I think they're a *little* better looking than we are," Callie laughed.

"Speak for yourself," Flint quipped. "But I agree, it's perfect. I think we're about to become millionaires. Can I get you a drink to celebrate? I'm thinking an old fashioned…"

"Is this the red-carpet treatment? A dip in the pool, a hastily made cocktail. I cannot believe that's all it takes to get these girls you invite over in bed."

"First of all, being with you would be like kissing my sister. Second, they're called women, Callie. Not girls."

She splashed water at him, and he hid the poster behind his back, keeping it safe.

"Oh, trust me, McQuaid. They're girls. Women, like me, know better."

"But you will take the drink?"

"I would love one, yes."

Just then, the phone rang. Flint hustled inside and emerged a moment later with a bright red rotary phone in his hands. The receiver was clenched between his jaw and his shoulder. The phone's long line allowed him to come up to the edge of the pool.

"Callie, I've got Weissbaum on the line. Noah, speak up, Callie's here with me."

Flint plopped down on the edge of the pool, dangling his legs into the warm water. He held out the receiver so they could both hear.

He asked, “So Noah, how are the test audiences?”

“Fantastic! Truly, they’re going wild for The Oak Island Enigma. I think you’ve both got something here. Bang up script, by the way, Callie. And you really proved yourself as a producer, Flint. I have to thank both of you.”

“Thanks, Noah,” Callie said.

“But you might say that the producer of the picture really made the script shine, Noah?”

Callie sucked pool water into her mouth and spat it out at Flint, who laughed and kicked at her, flinging water in her face.

“Cute, Flint. As always. But I’m actually calling with another proposition.”

“Ooh, do we get free popcorn at the premiere?” Flint said.

“I have a very tight schedule, McQuaid.”

“Sorry.”

“I actually read a very interesting article in the National Geographic Magazine today and it got me thinking.”

There was a pause on the other end of the line, and they heard Noah rattling ice about in a cocktail shaker. Flint mouthed the words *“Old fashioned”* at Callie and she nodded vigorously. They heard Noah pour the drink and he continued.

“It seems that a group of archaeologists exploring Mayan temples down in old Mexico have been vanishing. The locals claim that they’re being kidnapped and killed by a race of ancient ape men. Sounds quite a bit like that big hominid fellow that was reported up near Mt. St. Helen’s in Washington last year.”

The statement hung there in the air for a moment. Flint and Callie both knew what was coming next but knew better than to make assumptions about Noah's intentions.

"I was thinking," Weissbaum continued. "Maj. Roy is feeling pretty well again. A little worse for wear, but up and moving. I was thinking you might want to go and take a look, see what all the fuss is about. You probably won't have to deal with any Nazis this time around and I could see you getting a nice little three picture sequel deal out of it."

The phone hung in Flint's slack hand. He turned to Callie. They locked eyes, dumbfounded. Weissbaum's voice squawked through the phone.

"Well? How about it? Am I booking these plane tickets or not?"

The End

Will Flint take Weissbaum up on his offer to investigate? Will Flint and Callie find more than mutual respect? And could Declan have survived? All this and more will be answered in the next Flint McQuaid Adventure...

Showdown in the Yucatan

www.ingramcontent.com/pod-product-compliance
Lightning Source LLC
Chambersburg PA
CBHW061242170626
46809CB00007B/2795

* 9 7 8 1 9 2 2 8 6 1 7 5 7 *